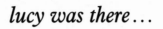

lucy was there...

lucy was there...

Jean Van Leeuwen

Phyllis Fogelman Books
New York

Published by Phyllis Fogelman Books
An imprint of Penguin Putnam Books for Young Readers
345 Hudson Street
New York, New York 10014
Copyright © 2002 by Jean Van Leeuwen
Designed by Lily Malcom
Text set in Granjon
Printed in the U.S.A. on acid-free paper
3 5 7 9 10 8 6 4 2

Library of Congress Cataloging-in-Publication Data
Van Leeuwen, Jean.
Lucy was there . . . / Jean Van Leeuwen.
p. cm.
Summary: With the help of new friends and a very special dog,
Morgan begins to come to terms with the loss of her mother and
five-year-old brother, who boarded a plane and never came back.
ISBN 0-8037-2738-0
[1. Loss (Psychology)—Fiction. 2. Grief—Fiction.
3. Friendship—Fiction. 4. Dogs—Fiction.
5. Family problems—Fiction.] I. Title.
PZ7.V3273 Lu 2002
[Fic]—dc21   2001033974

For Elizabeth

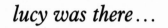

lucy was there . . .

one...

Lucy came first on a Tuesday late in the afternoon.

I was lying on my bed doing homework but not really. My math book was open with all the numbers lined up in rows. Sharp black and neat. Only when I looked at them they didn't stay that way. They blurred and swirled and tap-danced right off the bright white page. They wouldn't stay still long enough for me to figure out what to do with them. I know it wasn't my eyes needing glasses or anything. It was just my brain not able to wrap itself around them.

My brain wasn't wrapping itself around much of anything lately. And math was the first to go. Not that it had ever really come to me to the great disappointment of my father the math whiz.

The house was quiet as always. My father at work of course and Cassie doing whatever she did every day after school. Rehearsing for the spring musical most likely or else driving around in cars with boys with same-sounding names like Greg and Todd and Drew.

Cassie was either not home or on the phone.

Not home or on the phone. That was a poem and about all there was to say about my sister Cassie nearly sixteen and soon to be driving herself. Maybe she would drive herself right away from this house. I wouldn't be surprised. And then how quiet would it be?

So I was lying there on top of my quilt my great-grandmother had made before I was born. Pink and blue and yellow with little girls in sunbonnets on it worn to just-right softness. Even though the late-afternoon sun was slanting warm into my room I wrapped myself up in it just to feel the softness that was nowhere else in my life. And I must have fallen asleep though it didn't feel like it. Because there is no way to tell this other than a dream.

The first thing was only a feeling. Like someone else was in the room even though I knew no one else was in the house. Whatever was there felt big and it felt warm and I wasn't the least bit afraid which I usually am.

Afraid of thunder and lightning and snakes and

things that could be hiding under my bed waiting to grab me by the ankle. Afraid of too much quiet like this house.

In my dream or whatever it was I opened my eyes then and I saw Lucy. I knew right away that was her name. The same name as my great-grandmother but I don't think it is related. Because Lucy was a dog. A great big furry light-brown dog.

I'd always wanted a dog. For years and years. A dog would be my best friend I knew it. My dog would be waiting for me when I got home from school and we would do everything together even sleep curled next to each other on my bed at night. But there were always reasons why I couldn't have one. Not right now. Not while the baby is so little. Not until you are older and can take care of it yourself. But for the past few months after what happened I hadn't asked. I hadn't even thought about it.

So I was surprised to see Lucy even in a dream.

She had a kind face. That was the next thing I noticed. Her mouth was turned up in a smile which sounds strange but is true. A sweet gentle doggy kind of smile. A no-matter-what-you-do-I'm-going-to-keep-smiling kind of smile.

One of her ears turned up and one turned down giving her a look of being surprised. Her nose was velvety black. And then there were her eyes.

Her eyes were a glowing yellow with big black pupils. Black like the deepest darkest pools of water. Eyes you could fall right into it seemed like. But if you did fall in you wouldn't sink. You would come up and swim.

Right away I knew that. Lucy would hold me up.

Then I reached out to her and it seemed as if she reached out to me and she held me. Big and strong to lean against and so furry soft. I sank right into her.

"Lucy," I said.

Lucy the magic dog.

two...

What happened was this.

One day last November my mother and my little brother Ben went to visit my aunt Susan in Chicago.

My father and I drove them to the airport. Cassie being busy as usual said good-bye at breakfast.

Ben was so excited he bounced the whole way like a pink rubber ball. He was wearing that red baseball cap he always wore. He had his entire little-car collection in his backpack to show his cousin Adam which should have weighed him down but didn't seem to. And his scruffy bear with the smiley mouth named Fred sticking out between the straps.

All the way there in the car he asked questions.

How big would his airplane be?

Bigger than a fire truck?

Bigger than our house?

Bigger than an apartment house?

Could he sit up front with the driver?

Would he get to drive?

Did the airplane have windshield wipers in case it rained?

Would they see the ocean?

What if they bumped into a cloud? Would it be soft like a pillow?

Ben had never been on an airplane before.

At the airport he was wild. He ran all over the place while my mother and father stood in the long check-in line. I had to run after him grabbing at his backpack to slow him down. I started to wish I could tie him up with string into a package like some of the people in line were carrying. Flight attendants went by in their neat navy-blue uniforms pulling their neat wheeled bags and I felt sorry for the ones who would be getting Ben on their flight.

I sure hoped the flight to Chicago was on time. If he had to wait much longer he would explode.

And that was before he saw the planes all lined up outside the long windows like tied-up giant silver horses.

Ben's eyes got huge.

"Which one is my airplane?" he asked in a squeaky whisper.

Bouncing again. Jumping up and down. Grinning from one ear clear across to the other.

Finally we found out. We got to the gate and the flight was on time but we still had a half-hour to wait. My mother and father sat in the plastic seats with bags piled around their feet talking so quietly I couldn't hear what they were saying. Ben pressed his nose against the window glass looking out at his airplane.

His nose was stuck so tight I thought when it was time to board he might not get it unglued.

We sat like that for a long time while more and more people came with their bags crowding the seats and then suddenly words came crackling out of a microphone.

"Passengers on Flight 109 to Chicago may now begin the boarding process."

Ben bounced over and everything got in motion. People grabbing up their bags and moving toward the door that went to the plane. My mother hugging my father who was hugging Ben at the same time. Then giving me a quick smile and a hug.

"Take good care of Dad," she whispered in my ear.

Then she had Ben by the hand moving toward the door.

"Bye, Ben!" I called. "Have fun on your airplane!"

He turned around with a big grin and waved. The last I saw of him as he disappeared through the doorway was his bear Fred bouncing up and down in his backpack.

And that was the last I saw of my mother and my little brother from that day to this.

three...

Why would my mother do that?

That is my question.

Why would she run away from home and never come back or even call or write to see if we were okay? And take Ben with her too. Funny bouncy Ben who I still can see waving to me as he went through the doorway to his airplane. I want to know how he liked his first plane ride.

I don't understand it.

I thought she loved us. I thought she was happy with her life. Now that I think about it which I do all the time practically every minute of every day I remember things.

Like she and my father used to argue. Not too often. Well pretty often. But it was mostly just about little things like she forgot to buy the salad dressing that was the only kind he liked. Or she messed up her checkbook and he had to straighten it out. He was fussy (and still is but now no one can buy salad dressing for him but himself) and she forgot things. But it didn't seem to me like they were serious arguments. Sometimes they even ended up laughing.

Once or twice I heard her upstairs in her room crying though. So maybe they were really serious but I didn't know it.

Also I wonder if deep down inside my mother had secretly been wanting a whole different life and that is what she has gone to get.

"Take good care of Dad." That is what she said to me.

So maybe she had been planning it for a long time.

Instead of making cookies in the kitchen in her sweat suit she might be making lots of money in an office wearing a business suit. Or instead of driving us places like dance classes and soccer games and the mall which she hates she might be living in a little cabin in the mountains. Quiet and peaceful. Or on a farm. She used to talk about spending summers when she was little at her grandfather's farm in Vermont. Or maybe instead of giving piano lessons she decided to give concerts.

My mother plays the piano like you would hear on the

radio or TV. She is so good. She even went to music school instead of regular college and she won some kind of prize in a piano competition. Once I remember she told me that her teacher said she would go far.

Well she has gone far. Far away and never told us where.

Maybe I will read about her someday in the newspaper and she will be a famous piano player giving a concert at the White House or someplace like that. That would be something.

The worst thought that keeps creeping into my head before I can stop it is that she doesn't care about us anymore. Not my father or Cassie or me. The only one she couldn't bear to leave behind was Ben.

Which I can kind of understand because he is still so young only five and needs her.

But I need her too.

Then if I am not careful the worst thought of all sneaks in.

It is my fault. It was me who drove her away.

four...

I am not an easy child.

That is what I heard my aunt Susan say one time to my mother. They were sitting on the back porch having iced tea while Ben and Adam and Hallie and I played in the backyard. Only they didn't notice that I'd gone to the kitchen for a drink.

This was two years ago before Aunt Susan and Uncle Dan moved to Chicago.

"Morgan isn't an easy child, is she?"

Those were the exact words she used.

My ears must have stretched I was trying so hard to hear what my mother answered back. But I couldn't quite make it out.

"Oh, she's fine," she might have said. "No trouble at all."

That is what I would like to think.

Or it could have been, "Mm-hmmm." Said with a smile that meant she didn't really mind she liked me that way.

That would be all right too.

Or maybe she just shook her head all serious and frowning like she didn't know what she was going to do with me.

That is what I am afraid of.

If you aren't easy that makes you difficult.

I am not like my sister Cassie that is for sure. From the day she was born Cassie was always the perfect little girl. Sweet and smart and pretty with her long blond hair. She did her homework right on time in her oh-so-neat handwriting and her report cards always said "Gives her best effort." She did what she was told with-out arguing (which I never could) and hardly ever got into trouble (which I did pretty often). She even knows what she wants to be when she grows up. A dancer. She has been taking lessons just about forever and is really good.

So after Miss Perfect I must have come as a shock.

I like to climb trees and play baseball. When I was younger my knees and elbows were always skinned and scarred. Cassie's clothes that looked practically new when she handed them down to me would be wrecked in a week. By and large I don't like school because even though some of the teachers are nice like Mrs. Dixon last year others aren't. And you always have to do certain subjects at certain times no matter what. And even though I like reading and writing book reports and art I don't like math that I can't understand and social studies which is boring. On my report cards it always says "Doesn't work up to her potential."

My nice teacher Mrs. Dixon once called me a prickly person. That was when I was so busy with my picture of a monarch butterfly trying to get the colors just right that I didn't notice everyone else had moved on to spelling. When she spoke to me about it in her soft kind voice I answered (crankily I admit), "I never get to finish anything." Leaning over my desk she said in a whisper so no one else could hear, "Try not to be so prickly, Morgan."

Prickly like a cactus. Prickly like a porcupine. Thinking about it I kind of liked the thought of having all those prickles protecting me.

But I argue too much I know. It's just that I like to figure out things for myself not have someone else tell me.

And when I really want something like I wanted a dog so badly all those years I don't give up. I just keep asking. My father used to say I was stubborn. But my mother said no she's just determined. Which is really the same thing only a nicer way of saying it.

My mother said she first knew I was going to give her trouble when I was only two years old. She was showing me some pictures in my farm book and she pointed to a horse and said, "Horsie."

"Cow," I said.

"No, no," she said. "Horsie."

"Cow," I said.

She pointed to a cow on the next page and very carefully explained the difference to me.

"So you see, Morgan," she said, "that is a horse."

"Cow," I said.

My mother always laughed when she told that story.

But I don't know. I am not easy. I am difficult and stubborn and determined. And prickly as a porcupine.

I'm afraid it is all my fault she is gone.

five...

I wish I had someone to talk to.

I used to have friends but not now. Not real ones. My best friend Maggie moved away last summer and then this happened with my mother and Ben and my kind-of friends started acting strange.

They said they were sorry and how awful it must be but then they didn't know what to say next. Melissa looked down at her feet. Jen whispered something to Kristin. And then they had to go. "My mother is taking us shopping," Melissa said.

Mother.

"Oh!" She clapped her hand over her mouth. "Oh, I'm sorry."

The word *mother* is not permitted in my presence anymore.

Everyone at school is nice to me. The teachers too. Maybe too nice even. But they are nice from a distance. They look at me with I'm-sorry eyes and seem to be whispering It's-too-bad things as they pass by. No one asks me to go shopping though or to the movies on Friday night.

Not that I would go. I don't want to try on a bunch of clothes and hear what the right things are I should be wearing. And I don't care if Tim and Tommy and Brian who are the cutest boys in our class are sitting four rows in front of us and I wouldn't move to sit behind them either.

I think I have suddenly gotten old.

It would be good to talk to someone though. So last night I tried my father.

He was reading his newspaper in the den before dinner the same as always. It covered his face. That is how he has been since my mother left. Covered up. Behind something. His job at the bank mostly. And after dinner and on weekends down in his shop in the basement fixing things. He could fix anything. You could say it was his hobby. Fixing things that probably weren't even broken. He has always been like that. Busy and far away. Only now it is more.

"Dad," I said.

"Hmmm?" He didn't put down the paper.

What could I ask him? Something easy to start I figured.

"How is everything at the bank?"

"Fine." Still behind the business section.

"Is the new secretary okay?"

"Mm-hmm."

This was going well. Three words so far.

"Are you going to plant tomatoes this year?"

My mother just loved tomatoes. She filled up half our small backyard with them. She and my father had a little ceremony every spring. My father dug up the dirt and raked it and she planted. She grew so many tomatoes that the last half of the summer we had them with everything. Even fried for breakfast sometimes.

"No," he said quick and loud. He did put the paper down then. His face looked like I had hardly ever seen it. Pinched as if hit by a sudden pain.

He took a deep breath and said, "I can't do that."

I nodded. I could never eat them anyway. I just wanted to make him talk to me.

After dinner which was so quiet now without Ben I tried Cassie.

I knew I had to move fast before she got away.

"I'll help you clean up," I offered. She and I have a deal. She makes dinner (frozen mostly except for once in a while real spaghetti and once chili so hot my father said smoke was coming out of his ears—we laughed that night) and I vacuum (but only when I see dust balls in every corner).

She looked surprised.

"Thanks, Morgan."

So I started putting dishes in the dishwasher while Cassie put away the food and I was just thinking about what I could say to start off when she beat me to it.

"Would you mind a whole lot finishing up? I have a rehearsal at seven-thirty and Sean is picking me up." Smiling in that way Cassie has that always makes it hard to say no.

My hopes took a nosedive to my toes.

I shook my head. "I don't mind."

"Thanks a lot. You're the very best sister I have!" Old joke from our dim past. She dropped the sponge in the sink and ran upstairs.

I stayed in the kitchen scrubbing things that didn't

need scrubbing until she was gone and my father was down in the basement. Then I went up to my room to write to Maggie.

When she moved to New Mexico which she hated we said we would write to each other every week. And we did for a while. Then it got to be every other week and now it is more like every month. Her letters keep getting shorter and more cheerful. She likes it in New Mexico now and has a pecan tree right in her front yard. For Christmas she sent me a box full of nuts.

I had so much to say to her only it was really hard getting started.

"Dear Maggie, Why did you have to move away?"

That was no good.

"Dear Maggie, No one wants to talk to me."

That was terrible.

"Dear Maggie, I miss my mom and Ben."

Nothing sounded right when I wrote it down.

And she was so far away.

I crumpled up one piece of paper after another until the floor around my bed was covered with scrunched white balls.

Tears started in my eyes.

That was when Lucy came again.

It happened exactly the same. First an odd feeling of

someone being there. But nothing to be afraid of. No. Instead something filling up all of the empty space in my room. And then she was sitting at the foot of my bed just as big as before with those spooky dark eyes and that mysterious smile.

"Lucy," I said.

I was really crying now. It came pouring out of me how I missed my mother and funny little Ben in his red baseball cap and why did she do it and it wasn't fair to leave us and it must be my fault.

"I know it is," I said burying my face in my pillow.

The mattress creaked as Lucy settled herself next to me. She was warm so furry warm and soft it felt like I was melting right into her.

For the first time I heard her speak. Her voice was low and growlly like a dog's voice would be.

"It's all right," she said.

six...

Next door to us is a boy about Ben's age or I guess a little older. He is in first grade. His name is Alexander.

Alexander doesn't have a mother either. Not living in his house. She comes on weekends in her black shiny car and takes him away in the morning and brings him back at night.

During the week a baby-sitter Mrs. Briggs watches him after school. She is small and round with curly gray hair. Watches him is all she does from the kitchen window. She doesn't play with him. Alexander plays by himself in the backyard next to my backyard.

He used to always be playing with trucks in the dirt. Loading and unloading a yellow dump truck and putting out fires with his red fire truck. But lately he has been playing ball. Football last fall and now baseball. He throws the ball to himself. He has a pretend team that he talks to and I can hear him from our kitchen window. That is funny but also sad.

Alexander has sad eyes.

Yesterday I saw him from the window with a new red-brown baseball glove on his hand and it made me think of Ben in his baseball cap and I found myself walking out the back door.

"Want to play catch?" I asked him.

He was surprised but right away said, "Sure." Not smiling serious with dark hair falling down over big dark eyes.

I got the old glove that used to be my father's out of the garage. We played with a dirty yellow tennis ball throwing it back and forth in the grass in Alexander's backyard.

He was pretty good. He caught the ball *thunk* in his new glove almost every time.

Once in a while I would look up and see Mrs. Briggs watching us from the kitchen window that was just like ours except for the red checked curtains. She looked like she wasn't sure if this was a good thing or not.

I waved to let her know I was harmless and was not planning on kidnapping Alexander.

She didn't wave back but left the window.

So we kept on throwing *thunk thunk thunk* pretty hard now. I gave him a few high fly balls and he gave me some crazy ones I had to run for. We didn't talk except sometimes to say "Sorry" when my throw went over his head or "Nice catch."

Finally Alexander threw one up as high as he could.

The sun was in my eyes. I shaded them with my glove looking for the ball against the bright sky.

I backed up. Backed up some more. For a little kid Alexander could really throw. I was almost to the wall of our garage.

I stuck up my hand and the ball bounced off my glove and rolled into the grass.

"You got me that time," I said picking it up.

I saw that Alexander was smiling.

Then I felt my own face tugging in a way it wasn't used to and knew that for the first time in a long time I was smiling too.

seven...

Alexander is a funny boy.

He asks so many questions. Like Ben which made my throat catch only Alexander is different.

The thing about him is he is crazy about one subject and that is all he wants to know about. Last year it was trucks and now it is baseball. Every day when we play catch in his backyard he asks me a million questions.

Like do you have to be short to play shortstop?

I don't know.

I never thought about it. But now that he has brought it up I wonder who ever thought of such a weird name anyway.

And what is the infield fly rule?

I have no idea.

"Flies aren't allowed to buzz around the players' ears in the infield," I say trying to make a joke.

Alexander doesn't smile. He is always serious.

"No," he says. "That isn't right. It has to do with fly balls."

He watches baseball games on TV and that is where he gets all these questions.

His latest one is can he be a pitcher and a home run hitter at the same time?

After Alexander went out with his mother last Saturday he came home with a book about baseball. A big fat one with a lot of color pictures called *All About Baseball*. He showed it to me. In his new book he has been reading about the old-time players like Lou Gehrig and Babe Ruth who was a pitcher and a great hitter both.

"I don't think so," I told him.

"Why not?" he asked of course.

"Pitchers don't play every day," I pointed out. "Some of them don't even come up to bat. So you wouldn't get that many chances to hit all those home runs."

Alexander thought that over for a minute.

"I know what," he said. "I'll be an outfielder when I'm not pitching."

He has big dreams. I didn't have the heart to discourage him.

So we practiced pitching with a piece of old broken board as home plate and I had to be the umpire and call balls and strikes. Then we practiced hitting home runs with his red plastic bat and ball that made a great big *clunk* when you hit it. And after that we practiced catching fly balls in the outfield throwing the tennis ball higher and higher sometimes even into the branches of the big maple tree.

One time it got stuck up there and we had to go find a new ball.

I would have to say Alexander is best at catching and second best at pitching. He hasn't hit too many home runs yet. (A home run has to go over the garage or across the driveway into my yard either one.)

The thing about Alexander is he will keep on trying. He will keep on trying forever.

This is a good quality.

So maybe he can be a pitcher and home run hitter and outfielder all at the same time. Who knows? I wouldn't bet against it.

Mrs. Briggs seems pleased that Alexander has a friend and she doesn't have to watch him so much. She smiles at me now out the window while she is having a cup of tea at the kitchen table.

I am pleased too. Being friends with Alexander helps keep my mind off things.

eight...

Yesterday something peculiar happened.

It started on the school bus. It was raining. I was sitting next to the window looking at how the rain running down blurred everything outside so it looked like a painting. That French kind we learned about in art class. Blobs of running-together colors: green and gray and pink and white but mostly green. Light green. Bright green. All kinds of green. The title of this painting would have to be "Spring."

Behind me a couple of rows I could hear my used-to-be friends Melissa and Jen talking. Low so that people especially boys wouldn't hear but loud enough that I could catch enough words to know.

They were having a party.

It was this weekend. A sleepover it sounded like. At Jen's house for her birthday.

That would be right. Her birthday is in May.

"Makeup," I heard mentioned. Then "nail polish" and "restyle everybody's hair." Then some talk about what videos to rent. Some giggles and Jen's voice. "No, Tim, you're not invited."

I wasn't invited either. I knew that and I didn't care.

I didn't.

In my room in our house so quiet I could hear my own breathing I tried to do my homework about ancient Egypt.

But reading about that young queen closed up in her tomb with all those jewels and everything made me feel closed up too.

I couldn't breathe.

I had to get out of my room.

So I walked around in the hall hearing my own footsteps. And I made believe my mother was downstairs in the kitchen. She was moving around so quietly that I couldn't hear her but any minute now she would call up to me, "Cookies coming out of the oven!" I would run down and she would be there smiling. Come back to me.

Or Ben would come pounding upstairs with something probably all squashed in his little grubby fist to show me. "Look what I found!"

I listened hard.

Nothing but the *pat-pat* of rain on the hall window.

Cassie's bedroom door was closed as always with the *Swan Lake* poster sagging a little after being there so many years. She didn't like me to come in her room.

I turned the knob and walked in.

You wouldn't believe looking at Cassie so neat with her long blond hair done perfectly and clothes just right that her room could be such a mess. It always surprised me but it was. Like a tiny tornado had funneled in the window and struck just her room.

Clothes were everywhere. Ones she wore yesterday and a week or maybe even a month ago. On the bed. On the chair. In piles on the floor covering up her pink rug. Dripping out the closet door.

Besides the clothes there were school papers and books and magazines and dance programs. A bunch of stuffed animals. Dried-up awful-color roses that one of the same-sounding boys gave her on Valentine's Day. Parts of costumes that must be for the spring musical. A straw hat. Earrings and bracelets. Shoes. Dancing and regular.

Lined up almost neatly on her bureau were all her cosmetics. There must be ten thousand of them I thought. Bottles and tubes and little round jars of stuff I didn't know what all it was for. Well I did. Beauty. Making those boys want to take you out in cars and give you roses for Valentine's Day.

She had twenty-three different colors of nail polish. I counted.

Looking in Cassie's mirror I had a thought that sounded like words said out loud.

I did care about going to that party.

Well it isn't any use I answered myself. I stared back at my staring eyes. You're not going.

And it wouldn't matter anyway because no one could do anything about my hair that wasn't blond like Cassie's just dull brown and frizzed straight out the closer it got to summer. And my long face that had my father's chin. And my bitten-down nails.

I walked over to Cassie's closet door with the full-length mirror on the inside and looked at the full-length me.

Where Cassie was nicely rounded I was flat. Where she was curved I was straight. Where she filled out her clothes mine hung on me like a sack on a stick.

I must be the thinnest person in the entire world.

Skinny as a pencil.

Flat as a post.

A mess.

It was good I wasn't going to that party.

nine...

I had a dream.

It started out happy. I was flying. Not in an airplane but I had my own little set of wings stuck onto my shoulders. Kind of like a bee.

I was having a great time flying around in the bright sun and blue sky. And the best part was my mother and Ben were there too and we all had these same little wings.

We buzzed around each other smiling and laughing.

We did little helicopter tricks landing and taking off again straight up.

We could even turn upside down and still keep floating like being weightless in space.

Taking a nice little space walk.

Ben was laughing and bouncing around in that excited way of his. "Look at me! Look what I can do!"

My mother just kept smiling and smiling. She had the nicest most loving smile in my dream.

And I was so happy being with them again. I felt happy all over. I was so happy I turned a somersault.

But then when I looked up they were gone. Flying away into a great big cloud growing smaller and smaller.

Of course I flew after them only now my wings didn't seem to be working properly. I couldn't go fast or turn like before. My shoulders felt strange. And then I looked back and saw that my wings had fallen off.

I couldn't fly anymore.

Everything was bad all of a sudden.

My mother and Ben were gone and I was falling. Down and down out of that bright blue sky into scary dark.

I was crying and calling my mother to come back oh please please come back and there was a hole in my stomach.

And then suddenly Lucy was there. Lucy strong and sturdy right underneath me.

I landed lightly on her back holding tight to her soft fur.

She didn't say anything but I knew. I was safe. Lucy had me.

She was bigger than ever like a great gentle smiling brown bear. Like the bear in a story I couldn't quite remember that my mother used to read to me at bedtime.

And I rode on Lucy's back all the way to my bed.

ten...

This weekend while the party I wasn't invited to was going on I made myself over.

I went into Cassie's room again while she was out at the movies with the Valentine's Day boy. Sean his name is. I guess he is her boyfriend. He is tall and freckly blond and doesn't talk much and has a very old red car with fancy polished silver wheels.

I borrowed some of her ten thousand beauty products and also her beauty magazines and went into the bathroom. And when I came out I was a new person.

Kind of.

Partly.

I couldn't do anything about my hair. Or my pencil body. But I worked on my eyes and my nails.

One time a few months ago Cassie of the perfect hair looked at me and said with a little sigh, "Oh, I wish I had your eyes." I was so stunned at this I didn't know what to say. First that with the best hair in the world she could want anything else. And also that anything about me could be good enough to wish for.

After she said that though I studied myself in the mirror and I thought maybe I saw what she meant. My eyes were big (or maybe it was just that I was staring so hard) and blue like an oceany color. Cassie's were more gray.

So maybe I do have one good feature.

Just maybe.

Only one though.

In Cassie's latest issue of *Allure* magazine on the foot of her bed was an article called "When Your Eyes Are Your Best Feature." It was advertised on the cover. This was exactly what I needed like it was written for me. I followed the article's suggestions for using eye shadow and mascara to emphasize the eyes using Cassie's little jars and tubes.

The mascara applicator thing was weird like a strange twisted brush. It made me blink to touch my eyelashes.

But it worked. My eyes looked really bigger I thought. And bluer. A little smudgy underneath though.

This was great. It was easy making yourself over. Like an artist making a painting.

So I decided to give myself fingernails.

You don't have to bother growing your own nails anymore. You can just glue on fake ones. Of course Cassie had those too in her top drawer. I helped myself to a full set. Next time I go to the drugstore I will pay her back.

It felt odd having real (though fake) long fingernails. I had been biting mine as long as I could remember and more lately. My mother used to give me a manicure and paint my nails with pretty pale-pink polish on the theory that then I wouldn't want to bite them. And it kind of worked. For a while anyway. But then I would get all nervous about a math test or something and I couldn't help myself I'd start nibbling. And before I knew it they would be all bitten off again.

My new nails were so long. They felt strange like my fingers had grown about an inch overnight. I could tap them on the furniture and they made a nice clicking sound. I decided not to trim them at all.

Now I had to decide what color to paint my new nails. Cassie had so many to choose from. I took a few bottles to my room and tried them out sitting on my bed.

I liked the bright orange. And the silver. And the grapey purple so dark it looked almost black. She had bright red like a traffic light and white that looked like drops of pearls and even dark blue.

I alternated those three on different fingers to see how they looked.

Actually that looked kind of great.

Why not? I thought.

Why not go to school Monday as a new made-over person?

The old one wasn't doing so well.

I took off my red-white-and-blue nails and wiped my eyes with tissues and water until they weren't gloppy anymore. I put everything back in Cassie's room so carefully I didn't think she would know I'd been in there. That wasn't so hard with her room being such a mess.

Still I did feel a little sneaky which I'm not usually.

On Monday morning as soon as Cassie left early for school and my father called "Good-bye" up the stairs I went back to her room.

I did my eyes and nails again and went to school a new person.

eleven...

Well it didn't work out quite the way I thought.

On the bus this big loudmouth boy in my class Eddie Gallagher leaned across the aisle and said, "Hey, Morgan. Isn't it a little early for the Fourth of July?"

I didn't know what he was talking about and then his stupid friend Kevin said, "Real patriotic fingers you've got."

The two of them had a good laugh while I folded my hands in my lap so my fingernails wouldn't show.

Melissa and Jen and Kristin were busy talking at the back of the bus about their party so they didn't hear. But then getting off Jen looked at me and said, "What happened to your eye?"

She was serious. Not like Eddie Gallagher. She thought I had a black eye or something.

"Nothing," I said quick so no one else would look. Maybe I put too much of that eye shadow stuff on one eye when I was hurrying to catch the bus.

But they were all three looking now. Melissa had her hair different I noticed pulled back in some kind of fancy braid and they all had on dark purple nail polish.

All one color though.

"See you later," I said.

I went down the steps in a hurry and off to the classroom as if I had something important to do and was late already.

Behind me I could hear them still talking and laughing. Maybe about the party. Maybe about me.

I hadn't counted on Mrs. Deeley my this-year's teacher. She has eyes like a hawk and even looks like one with her bony body and gray pinned-back hair and beaky nose. Mrs. Deeley never smiles. She likes to catch people doing things they shouldn't be doing while she is talking and make them turn all red in the face. Make them read out loud the note they were passing to a friend. Or show what they are hiding in their desk that isn't allowed in school. That is her greatest pleasure I think.

She is so the opposite of my last-year's teacher Mrs.

Dixon who looks like a round fuzzy peach and smiles all the time.

Anyway I was first in the classroom because I'd been hurrying so much pretending to have something to do. That was a big mistake. Because Mrs. Deeley looked me slowly up and down with her sharp hawk eyes and said, "Morgan."

"Yes?" I had my eyes looking straight down at my desk and my nails curled up inside my hands.

It was no use.

"Let me see your left eye."

She came straight to my desk and put one bony finger under my chin tipping my head up. "It looks like you've had an accident."

I knew what she really meant. She thought I'd been in a fight or maybe something worse than that like child abuse.

I shook my head. "It's nothing. Just makeup."

She ought to be able to tell with those sharp eyes.

"Look." I reached in my pocket for a tissue to rub it off but Mrs. Deeley didn't give me a chance. She had me standing up and going out the door just as everyone else was coming in.

"You go down to the nurse's office and let her take a look," she said.

The really worst thing about Mrs. Deeley is she never believes what you say.

The nurse Mrs. Martin was nice. She asked a lot of questions but she looked like she believed my answers.

She wanted to know how I managed to get myself a black eye.

Uh-oh. Here came the fight or child abuse thing again.

"It's not a black eye," I told her. I got water and paper towels from the sink and showed her it came off.

"Well, that's a relief." She smiled.

She sounded a little like my mother.

I told her it was my sister's eye makeup and Mrs. Martin said next time I should ask my sister to help me.

"Sometimes less is more," she said.

I had the feeling she might be talking about my nails too but she didn't mention them.

"I guess so," I answered.

She had me sit still while she cleaned up my eyes and even rubbed in some good-smelling cream.

"Thank you," I said.

It was time to get back to class. But when I started to stand up she asked, "How are things at home?"

That is the way they always ask. Not "How are you doing without a mother?" Or "Have you stopped listening for your little brother's voice?" Or "Are you feeling really mad or more sad that they went off and left you?"

People always have an embarrassed look when they ask too. Like they're not sure if they are saying too much or maybe too little. Even nice nurse Mrs. Martin.

I always answer the same way.

"Fine."

Usually they don't say anything more.

Mrs. Martin looked as if she wanted to say more. I stood on one foot and then the other waiting. I would have just left but it wouldn't be polite. My parents brought us up always to be polite.

"Black eye or no black eye," Mrs. Martin said finally smiling but serious, "you can always come and talk to me. If you want to."

I nodded. "Okay."

This whole makeover thing had been a disaster. The whole day was a disaster. And it was only 9:15.

I walked slowly back to the classroom practicing as I went how to hide my dumb Fourth-of-July nails by keeping my hands in fists.

All day I would do it. I wouldn't raise my hand or pass papers down the row. Or copy the vocabulary words from the blackboard.

Right.

It would never work.

In Mrs. Deeley's class there was no place to hide.

So I decided right then not to care. Let anybody laugh or whisper and it wouldn't bother me. I could take it.

I was all set to be that way at lunchtime when Isabelle Pratt sat down next to me.

"I love your nails," she said.

I looked at her.

"I mean it," she said. "Really. I think they're great."

Isabelle is an artist. Kind of different from everybody else with her carrot-colored hair and round moon face and the faded overalls she always wears. She is crazy about color. In art class she does peculiar paintings that don't look like anything but bright blobs of paint.

I could see from her eyes that looked right at me without blinking that she meant it. Probably Isabelle always told the truth.

"Thanks," I said.

Just at that moment the day didn't seem quite so bad.

twelve...

Alexander liked my fingernails.

"You look like a clown," he said. "You could maybe get a job in the circus."

Alexander's mother had taken him to see the circus in New York City a few weeks back.

A little frown screwed up his face.

"But long fingernails aren't good for ballplayers," he said.

He was right about that. Long fingernails got in the way of doing things I had discovered. Also they felt funny.

"I'll be right back," I told him.

I went across the driveway to my house and went upstairs and took off the fake fingernails. I felt better with just my own stubby chewed ones. My hands seemed lighter.

"Let's play ball," I said.

Alexander must have been reading his baseball book because today his questions were all about Babe Ruth.

"Did Babe Ruth really play at Yankee Stadium?"

I nodded. "I think so."

"The same Yankee Stadium they have now?"

"Right," I said.

"In New York City?"

"Yes."

"Wow."

For a few minutes we just threw the ball.

Then Alexander asked, "Who was president when Babe Ruth was playing? Abraham Lincoln?"

"No," I said. I didn't know who it was though.

His face had that thinking-hard look again.

"I don't think it was George Washington," he said.

"Definitely not."

I had to smile. When you are in first grade you don't learn about any other presidents. Just Washington and Lincoln like they were the only two. No wonder he was mixed up.

"There were lots of other presidents," I told him. "I'll find out which one and let you know."

A few more minutes went by.

"When Babe Ruth was playing do you think they had ice cream?"

I tried to remember pictures of the olden days at ballparks I'd seen on TV. Were people in the stands eating ice cream in those pictures? I didn't remember it. But they must have had ice cream. Ice cream has been around pretty much forever.

"I think so," I said. "Sure they did."

Alexander looked pleased. "Good."

I knew what he meant. Somehow it wouldn't be right to have baseball without ice cream.

"No TV though," I said.

"I know."

Just then I had the best idea for Alexander.

"You know what you could maybe do? You could ask your mom to take you to a baseball game at Yankee Stadium."

Alexander stopped throwing the ball.

"Do you think she would?" he asked.

"Maybe." It seemed like his mother since she left would take him about anywhere. "Or your dad," I added. "This summer sometime you could go to a game."

Alexander nodded. He was trying not to get too excited. But he couldn't help it his feet were practically dancing in the grass.

"I'll ask her. Oh, boy! I could see where Babe Ruth stood when he hit all those homers."

Inside my head was a question that had been there for a long time. Without warning it came leaking out.

"How is it to have a mom just on weekends?"

Alexander looked down at his sneakers. Scuffed white ones with blue lightning things on the sides. He didn't say anything.

I wished I hadn't asked.

"Okay," he said finally. "It's kind of good. She takes me a lot of places we never went before. And she got me that baseball book."

"That was really nice."

"Yeah."

He was looking at his sneakers again like he was talking to them.

"But I don't like it in the night."

thirteen...

I don't like it in the night either.

Dreams keep coming. Flying ones again or else dark shadowy ones that I can't quite remember but that wake me up scared. My heart beating *brr-umm brr-umm brr-umm* loud in my chest.

In one dream my mother was putting a bandage on my knee the way she used to do all the time when I was little. I was always skinning my knees. I sat in her lap and her arms were around me safe and warm and she was talking softly so I wouldn't notice how much it hurt. She could even make me smile sometimes with her silly talk.

She would ask me riddles. My mother loved riddles. Especially the ones about the elephant in the refrigerator. She'd be laughing before she even finished asking the riddle.

This was a good dream. Inside my dream somehow I knew that and I didn't want to wake up. I wanted to stay that way forever.

Listening to my mother's voice.

With her arms around me.

I smiled up into her face. And it wasn't hers at all. It was that school nurse Mrs. Martin's face.

"Mom!" I cried.

Up and up I swam out of that dream and there was a deep black hole inside me and I was holding on to my pillow as if it was her and crying.

I cried until nothing was left inside my head.

Then I opened my eyes and I saw Lucy.

This time she was stretched out across the bottom of my bed like a small mountain. She looked comfortable and kind of sleepy.

"It was only a dream," she said exactly the way my mother used to when I had a bad dream in the night. Only Lucy's voice was different low and rumbly.

I could feel myself slowing down getting calmer inside.

"She was here," I whispered.

Lucy lifted her head and looked at me with those dark wet wise eyes of hers.

"I felt her," I said. "I heard her voice."

She seemed to nod her large head.

"If only I could hear her voice again really."

Lucy didn't say anything. The room was still. And dark except for the dim glow of the streetlight through the yellow daisy curtains my mother had made.

I wasn't sure if the words came from her or from inside my own head but I heard them.

"Maybe you can."

fourteen...

I would call my aunt Susan in Chicago that's what I'd do.

But what would I say?

"I need to hear my mother's voice." (Please Aunt Susan help me.)

And what would she say?

"I'm sorry, Morgan. But I don't know how to reach your mother."

"That's not true. You do. I'm sure of it. If anyone in the world can reach her, it's you."

I can't say that. It's too rude.

My parents brought us up never to talk back to an adult. According to them it is the worst thing a child can do practically.

Whatever I say I have to be polite.

And can I even stand to hear Aunt Susan's voice? It is so much like hers husky and soft so you almost have to strain your ears to make out the words. Only my mother's always sounded like she had just finished laughing.

Sounds.

I can do this. She is my aunt after all my mother's sister and she cares about us. Sometimes she calls my father late at night and they talk for a long time. I don't know what they talk about. He never says.

My father is a very quiet man. I hadn't really realized that before my mother left. She was the one who always did the talking.

So what time should I call Aunt Susan?

I have to allow for the one-hour time difference. And I want to get her on the phone not Uncle Dan or Hallie or Adam.

She works in the mornings at some house-selling place so that is no good. Anyway I am at school then.

Most likely she'd be home at five-thirty fixing dinner. But that would be our eating time. And anyway she would probably have something cooking on the stove and the kids yelling in the next room so she couldn't give me her full attention.

I need her full attention.

Three o'clock her time is probably the best bet. Just before the school bus comes if it comes the same time as ours so she is pretty sure to be there.

Four o'clock my time. That is when I will call.

Tomorrow.

So I got off my bus at three-twenty and I told Alexander I couldn't play with him today I had something to do.

"Oh," he said his face falling about a mile. "I was going to practice my curveball."

Alexander does not have a curveball. But he is hoping to get one.

"Tomorrow," I said.

"Okay."

I fixed myself some crackers with peanut butter and jelly and ate them remembering the snacks my mother used to have waiting for me. Just-baked oatmeal cookies or sometimes even chocolate chip. Or else some healthy fruit or carrot sticks cut in funny shapes.

Not that she did that every day I had to keep reminding myself. Because looking back now it seemed like every day. Sometimes I know she was busy giving a piano lesson or just playing the piano herself and she forgot to make any snack at all.

After my snack it was 3:35.

The kitchen clock moved so slowly like it was too

steep a climb for that tired old minute hand to get all the way to the top.

The second hand kept zipping around though.

"If the little hand is on the three and the big hand is on the eight, what time is it? Don't tell her now, Cassie." That was the game my mother and I used to play when I was four or five.

I called it The Clock Game and I had my own little red cardboard clock with hands that moved. I used to practice for hours.

"Can we play The Clock Game?" I would ask.

The big hand was now on the nine and the little hand had crept nearly to the four.

I stood up. I got a glass from the cupboard and went to the refrigerator and took out the milk carton and poured myself a glass of milk and put back the milk carton and sat down.

All just as slowly as I possibly could.

That took less than a minute.

I drank the milk. Swallow. Rest. Swallow. Look at the glass with the faded yellow flowers on it. Swallow. Look down at my fingernails that I was trying again to grow.

Do not bite those fingernails whatever you do.

Three-forty-eight.

Okay do I have to wait until exactly four? Aunt Susan

could just as easily be there right now. And if she isn't I can hang up before the answering machine switches on.

I picked up the phone and punched in the number I knew by heart. My fingers seemed to be shaking for some reason.

She wouldn't be there. And even if she was she wouldn't tell me how to reach my mother. My mother didn't want to be reached. Even by her own children.

That was the awfulest thing.

"Hello?"

It was Aunt Susan.

My throat closed up and I couldn't say anything.

"Hello?" A pause. "Is anyone there?"

My mother's voice but not quite.

Not hers. Never hers.

My throat and my whole head were choking full of something bursting to get out. But I couldn't let it.

No I had to keep it in.

Click. I put down the phone.

fifteen…

My hair looked like a triangle.

It stuck straight out on the sides like two big bushes of frizz.

That was because it had been raining for three days in a row. The frizz was always worse when it rained.

But how could I go to my sister's spring musical looking like this?

I wandered into her room to ask her.

Well that was a mistake. Cassie was whirling around like her own little funnel cloud tossing stuff in every direction.

"I can't find it," she wailed when she saw me. "And I don't know my lines for Act Three and Abby's mom will be picking me up any minute and it's going to be a disaster."

"What can't you find?"

"The script. I had it last night so it has to be here. Somewhere."

Picking up a pile of clothes from the bottom of her bed she flung them in the air so it rained T-shirts and jeans.

Cassie was nervous. I was surprised. I always thought she was so sure about everything.

I walked over to the bedside table. No script there.

Leaning down I pushed aside her blanket that was dragging on the floor and there it was.

"Here." I handed it to her.

"Oh thanks, Morgan! You saved my life. Only now I don't have time to study it and just look at my hair."

Her hair looked perfect as always. Which reminded me.

"Look at mine," I said. "What can I do with all this frizz?"

She gave me two seconds of a glance.

"Hair spray," she decided. "Lots and lots of hair spray. Here, you can borrow mine."

She handed me a silver can. Then a car honked outside and Cassie went into a major twirl around the room picking up clothes and hair things and the script and cramming them all into a bag.

"Wish me luck," she said.

"Good luck. Not that you need any," I told her. "You'll be great."

She flashed me half a smile and off she went pounding down the stairs.

A minute later she came pounding back up.

"Shoes!" She grabbed her dance shoes and was gone again.

I heard the car drive away.

Whew. That was exhausting. I felt like lying down.

Instead I worked on my hair.

The first thing to do was get it to lie flat. I brushed it and put water on it and pressed it down hard with my hands. It kept trying to pop back up but I wouldn't let it. While I was holding down one side I sprayed it with a whole lot of hair spray just like Cassie said. Then I did the same thing with the other side.

Looking in the mirror I thought my hair looked kind of good. A little like I was wearing a helmet but that was okay. Better than two frizzy bushes on the sides of my head.

My father didn't say anything about my hair. I don't think he noticed.

We went to the spring musical by ourselves.

It still felt strange after all this time not to take up most of a row. And not to have Ben jumping up and down asking a million questions. He never could sit still and someone always had to be whispering to him. Or my mother would take him on her lap or my father would draw pictures for him on his program.

I wondered if my father was thinking about that.

I snuck little glances at him out of the corner of my eye.

He was sitting up straight and tall wearing his good jacket. Gray tweed. I always liked that jacket it looked so soft. Gray was in his light brown hair too that I didn't remember being there. Just at the sides like frosting. His mouth was set in a thin line and he stared straight ahead as if he didn't want to miss a single moment of Cassie's play even though it hadn't started yet.

My father was like a package tied up tightly with string. I couldn't even guess what was inside.

That reminded me of last Christmas. The first one without my mother and Ben.

It was the worst time.

My father tried hard to make it the same as always. He got the tree and put the lights on and Cassie and I hung the ornaments while we all listened to Christmas carols on the radio.

But my father when he didn't know you were looking looked so sad. And every ornament we put on reminded me of something. My mother at the kitchen table helping me paint those little wooden Santas. Ben's face when he brought home that weird macaroni wreath from nursery school. The bird's nest he found in the backyard that we always put on a low branch so he could look at it. My eyes kept filling up so I couldn't see where I was hanging them.

My father gave us too many presents. And all of Christmas Day I was listening for the telephone my ears stretched toward any little sound.

She didn't call. Not even on Christmas.

Finally at night Aunt Susan called but I couldn't talk to her.

The auditorium lights faded slowly to dark and the orchestra started playing and the curtain opened.

Cassie was on stage.

She wore a red checked dress with a puffed-out skirt and straw hat. And she was good. Right away you could see it. She sang in a small voice but right on key and she danced.

Oh she was a great dancer. She whirled around like she did at home but now it was to music. She made everybody else on stage who were only in the show for fun look like they were made of wood. Especially the boys. So much energy came bursting out of her that it seemed to spill over the edge of the stage into the audience.

My father was smiling. I could feel it without looking. So was everybody else in the auditorium.

No doubt about it. Cassie was the star of the show.

I could just see her a few years from now on Broadway. It could happen I knew it. That gave me a peculiar choked feeling in my throat. My sister knew where she was going. And she was going to go off and leave me.

At the end of the show Cassie got a lot more applause than anyone else. High school kids in the back were whistling and some people even stood up clapping. My father did so I did too.

My mother would have been so proud. She probably would have been whistling too. And Ben would be jumping up and down and waving at Cassie up on stage.

Why wasn't my mother here? She should be here for Cassie at least for this moment.

The applause that seemed like it would go on forever finally stopped.

"Wasn't she terrific?" My father was beaming. Really smiling for the first time in months.

"Fantastic," I agreed.

We went backstage and hugged Cassie who was glowing like a lightbulb had been turned on inside her face.

"Great job!" I told her.

"Wonderful!" my father said. "Everyone was wonderful."

"Thanks. I was so scared!"

So many people were crowded around her that we couldn't really talk.

"I'm going to the cast party at Abby's house," she said over her shoulder. "Sean will bring me home."

"Okay," answered my father.

Then she went off with a bunch of other kids to the cast party and my father and I went home.

He took off his tweed jacket and went down to the basement as usual and pretty soon I could hear hammering.

Loud and on and on like that applause. I kept hearing it even after I got in bed until finally it mixed together with a dream about dancing.

Some time later I woke up. The house was finally quiet. I looked at the clock radio next to my bed. One-forty.

Cassie must be home by now. Home and sleeping exhausted by all that dancing. Or maybe too excited by all that applause ever to sleep again.

I tried to go back to sleep.

But I kept seeing Cassie dancing off that stage and out of the house to Broadway.

I'd go get some warm milk to make me sleepy. That was the thing to do.

Cassie's door was closed. I couldn't hear anything behind it.

Going down the stairs I could see a dim light below. It was coming from the kitchen. My father or Cassie must have left it on by mistake.

Then as I passed the dining room I heard something.

A low muffled sound like moaning.

I stopped in the doorway my heart thumping in my ears.

It was my father making that terrible sound. He was slumped over the kitchen table with his head resting on his hands. He looked like all his bones had collapsed. His shoulders in the blue paint-spattered work shirt he always wore were shaking.

I had never seen my father cry.

I backed up my feet to get upstairs before he saw me. But he must have heard something and lifted his head.

"Morgan." That was all he said in a hoarse voice.

"Are you all right?"

Which was a silly question because for sure he wasn't.

He shook his head. "Tonight was hard."

I nodded.

"Sometimes I miss your mom and Ben so much."

Down deep somewhere I felt myself shudder. I couldn't talk my throat was so squeezed.

Instead I reached out my hand and touched his shoulder. I had never done that before.

My father pressed my hand so tight my fingers crunched together. Possibly broken I thought.

"Dad."

His eyes looking up were little-boy eyes.

"Will she ever come back?"

My father looked surprised. His eyebrows slanted together in a frown.

"You know she won't," he said.

You know she won't. She won't she won't she won't.

I heard his words over and over again as I climbed back into bed. He sounded so sure but how did he know? She will she will she will I said back to him. But then another thought came sneaking in. If she didn't come for something as big as Cassie's show maybe she really never would. No I argued. She will she will she will.

I lay flat on my back in the dark with those words

spinning around in my brain like I was on some merry-go-round that wouldn't stop. I will never sleep again I thought. Never in my entire life.

Lucy I called. I need you now.

And just like that Lucy came. She opened her big arms and folded me inside and held me tight.

Oh Lucy. Thank you.

I nestled close to her. She stroked my hair and murmured softly, "It's all right."

It wasn't really all right I knew. But with Lucy there it was better.

After a while my thoughts began to blur together willwon'twillwon't and then they collapsed and I was asleep.

sixteen...

I had to do something about my hair.

Now that it was June and starting to get hot it was worse than ever. Every morning I sprayed my entire head with hair spray. That worked for a little while. But even before I got off the school bus curls started escaping. I could practically hear them popping out. *Boing! Boing! Boing!* And by lunchtime my hair would be its wild frizzy self again only just a little stiffer.

I borrowed some of Cassie's beauty magazines to study the problem.

To judge by the articles (not to mention the advertisements) I am not the only person in the world afflicted by this condition.

The experts had lots of suggestions.

I should never ever brush my hair.

I shouldn't wash it too often to take out the natural oils.

I shouldn't dry it unless I had some kind of special hair dryer with a huge attachment that looked like a shower head.

I should use only certain hair care products like protein-conditioning cream and heat-activated gel and natural straightening balm and frizz-free styling mousse.

On humid days I could wear my hair in a ponytail if I did some fancy braiding thing that looked much too hard.

Or I could wear it smashed down and pulled back in a style that reminded me of Mrs. Deeley.

It was all very confusing. But I went to the drugstore and loaded up on all the hair care products and the hair dryer with the shower-head attachment which cost three whole allowances.

Then I tried everything out.

I don't know if it was those magazine articles just trying to make frizzy-haired people feel better or the hair care companies lying to get people to buy their products. Or if I didn't do something right following the directions. That could maybe be it.

All I know is I didn't see one bit of improvement.

None.

I stood at the bathroom sink looking in the mirror thinking what do I do now?

I am always going to be the girl wearing two bushes on her head.

Cassie would know what to do. She could tell me. If she was home. I walked across the hall and knocked on her door.

No answer.

Now I remembered. She had gone with her friend Abby to look at prom dresses.

I went to my room and looked in my desk drawer until I found some scissors. I took them back to the bathroom.

Should I or shouldn't I?

I could not stand this awful miserable hair one more minute.

I held out a piece on one side and—*snip!*—cut it off close to my head. There. That wasn't so hard. I took another snip. A bigger one. A few more. Then a few on the other side to make it even.

Now for the top.

Snip snip snip. Faster and faster I went. This was actually fun I thought. I could be a hairdresser someday.

Bush you are history.

The back was a little harder. I borrowed Cassie's hand mirror so I could see what I was doing but it just confused me seeing everything backwards. So I didn't look in the mirror. I held out a hunk of hair with one hand and hacked it off with the other.

My head was feeling lighter and lighter. It was amazing how all that hair had weighed me down. I should have done this a long time ago.

I kept on snipping until the sink was nearly full of dark clumps of hair. It looked like some kind of small furry animal lying there.

Finally I stopped.

I looked in the mirror and didn't recognize who was looking back. My head seemed smaller and my mouth bigger and my eyes suddenly huge.

I was a whole new person. If my mother came back she wouldn't recognize me.

But she was never coming back. My father said so.

So all in all this seemed like a good thing.

seventeen...

"What have you done to your hair?"

Cassie's mouth was open staring at me. She actually dropped her English muffin onto her plate.

"I don't believe it," she said. "Did you really try to cut it yourself?"

She was so amazed sitting there with her perfect long blond nonfrizzy hair. It made me mad.

"Sure," I said calmly drinking down my juice. "It was easy."

"What were you thinking of, Morgan? Really. Have you looked at the back?"

I hadn't but I didn't want to admit it.

"What's wrong with the back?"

"It looks like moths chewed on it while you were asleep." She shook her head her hair staying just where it should. "You'll have to go to Letitia's after school. She'll trim you up. I can take you over there if you want."

It was surprising that Cassie would take the time to go anywhere with me. Part of me wanted to say okay. But I could feel the other part stiffening up. The stubborn determined part.

"I don't know if I want it trimmed."

My father looked up from his coffee and newspaper. He hadn't said a word when I came downstairs so I didn't think he noticed.

"You want it trimmed," he said quietly.

Cassie jumped up cramming the rest of her muffin into her mouth. "Got to go. I'll be home after school if you want to go to Letitia's."

"Okay. Maybe."

I went upstairs and looked at the back of my hair in the mirror and decided to wear my baseball hat to school.

Alexander noticed right away even with the hat on.

"Where is your hair?" he asked on the bus.

"I cut it," I answered.

"That's good," he said. He looked me over carefully. "Now you look like a real ballplayer."

That was the biggest compliment coming from Alexander.

Mrs. Deeley though wouldn't let me keep on my hat in the classroom.

Of course. How could I have thought she would?

She looked right at me when I walked in and said in front of everyone, "Somebody seems to have forgotten that hats are not worn inside the classroom. Isn't that right, Morgan?"

Everyone turned around and looked at me of course. Twenty-two sets of staring eyes.

"Morgan. Did you hear me?"

Mrs. Deeley has a way of standing still looking at you with her see-everything eyes until you crumble inside.

I almost did. I could feel my stomach go hollow and my legs and arms start to turn to jelly. My hand reached up to take off my baseball hat. But then I surprised Mrs. Deeley and even myself.

"No," I said.

A kind of soft sigh floated across the room as if everyone was taking a deep breath at the same time. No one had ever talked back to Mrs. Deeley before not even Eddie Gallagher who always talked back. Not this whole school year. Chairs squeaked as kids sat straight up.

"I beg your pardon?" Mrs. Deeley's face looked like she couldn't believe her ears.

I couldn't believe mine either. What had I done? What was going to happen now?

I couldn't back down. My hand refused to go up and take off that hat. But I couldn't speak either. There was nothing more to say. Also my throat was closed so I could barely breathe.

Something had to happen. Tears burned my eyes as I jumped up from my desk and ran out of the room.

In the hallway I just stood leaning against the cool brick wall trying to calm down and not cry. If I started I might not be able to stop. No one else was in the hall. I could hear the usual far-off school noises though. Mr. Farrell in the next room droning on and someone playing a squeaky violin in the music room and glasses clinking in the cafeteria. It was like being in school but not being there.

I tried to imagine what would happen next. Would I have to go to the principal's office? Would they call my father? I had never been in real trouble before not one time since I started kindergarten.

"Morgan."

I turned around and Mrs. Deeley was there. This was

it then. Now I would find out what being in real trouble was like.

I tried to stand up straight to face the firing squad.

"Morgan," she said again. Her voice was softer than usual. She stopped. For the first time all year it seemed like Mrs. Deeley wasn't sure what to say.

"I—uh—I'm sorry we had this difficulty today," she said finally. Her eyes weren't quite looking at me. They appeared to be focused on the wall over my shoulder. "I know you've had some—some problems this year. So perhaps we should just forget this little incident."

I was so surprised I didn't know what to say.

"You may keep the hat on," she went on starting to sound like herself again. "Just this once to hide your hair. Do we understand each other?"

She knew about my hair. But she wasn't going to humiliate me in front of the whole class. This was amazing and strange.

All I could do was nod my head.

"Good," she said in her old brisk Mrs. Deeley way. "Now you'd better get back inside for the vocabulary test."

All morning I felt eyes staring at me as if I was someone new no one had noticed before. I heard whispering from the desks behind me. Jen and Kristin most likely.

And Eddie Gallagher leaned across the aisle and said under his breath, "Way to go!"

"Edward?" Mrs. Deeley wheeled around from the blackboard. "Did you have something to say to the class?"

His ears turned bright pink. "No," he mumbled trying to shrink his big self under his desk.

At lunchtime I was the center of attention. People crowded around my table congratulating me as if I'd just done something fantastic like flown to the moon. Jen and Kristin wanted to know what I'd said to Mrs. Deeley out in the hall. Eddie and Kevin and Tim wanted to know if I thought it would be okay for them to wear their Yankee hats tomorrow.

"I wouldn't recommend it," I told them and they nodded like I was the world's living expert on Mrs. Deeley.

It was odd having everyone look at me and hang on every word I said. This must be what it feels like to be a movie or rock star.

Finally things started quieting down. People drifted off to other tables to eat their lunch.

"That was brave of you," said Isabelle Pratt.

I hadn't noticed with everyone milling around talking that she was sitting at the end of the table.

"Not really," I answered. I hadn't planned it after all or even known I was going to do it. It just sort of happened.

"Yes it was," she said as if she knew something about me I didn't know myself.

I felt mixed up. People were acting like I was some kind of hero. But I'd been rude to an adult and even worse a teacher. My mother would not be pleased if she heard about it. Neither would my father who might be hearing about it soon. But then again it wasn't right for a teacher to make you feel about two inches tall. Something stubborn in me had drawn a line and said it wasn't going to happen this time.

"Well maybe," I said.

For a few minutes we just ate our lunches and then Isabelle said, "So what did you do to your hair? Cut it yourself?"

I stared at her. Was it that obvious?

"I did that last year," she said. "I was so mad at my stupid hair I cut it all off. Really. I looked like a boy. Don't you remember?"

I really didn't remember Isabelle much from last year. Now her hair looked great though. Short and curly all over. Like a Raggedy Ann doll I thought being carroty red but I didn't say it.

"I murdered mine," I told her. "My sister says it looks like moths chewed up the back."

Isabelle peeled her orange. Carefully she arranged the

peels in a circle around the edge of her plate. She looked like she wasn't sure if she wanted to say something.

Finally she said looking down at the peels, "If you want I could fix it up for you after school. My mom works in a beauty shop. She's been teaching me to cut hair."

I wasn't sure either what to say. I could go home and meet Cassie and she would take me to Letitia's to have it trimmed.

"Okay," I said.

eighteen...

Isabelle and I got to be friends while she was cutting my hair.

"Moths?" she said snipping away at the back with her mother's long hair-cutting scissors. "I'd say it was more like a plague of locusts back here."

That got me laughing remembering Mrs. Deeley explaining about those awful insects that ate up all the crops and everything else in sight back in ancient Egypt times.

Then we started talking about Mrs. Deeley. How mean she was especially to the boys. What made her that way. What happened to Mr. Deeley if there ever really was one which was hard to believe.

"He died from discouragement," said Isabelle.

"Or ran away with that pretty young kindergarten teacher from last year," I suggested. "Now he's living on the beach in California."

We laughed some more and before I knew it Isabelle was brushing the itchy hair off my neck and saying, "Voila! The new you."

I looked in her bathroom mirror and I didn't know myself. My hair was all evened out and close to my head in kind of soft waves. No trace of frizz anywhere which was shocking. My eyes did look bigger and somehow bluer and even more amazing my whole face had a shape now. I looked like a more definite person. Neat and trimmed. Put together. Feet on the ground not fly away into the sky like I used to be.

This was strange.

"You look really different," Isabelle told me holding up a hand mirror so I could see the back.

"Different good?"

"Definitely. Great in fact."

"Well you did a great job."

"I've been cutting my brothers' hair for two years," Isabelle explained. "My mom's too busy to do it ever since she bought the beauty shop. I do my dad's too but that's easy because he doesn't have much."

While she was talking she was putting away things and sweeping up the dark wisps of hair on the floor like they do in a real beauty shop.

I looked around at her bright pink and green bathroom. Everything matched. Towels and rug and tiles and shower curtain and tissue-holder and toothbrush-holder and wastebasket. Giant pink flowers and swirling green vines were painted on the walls. I'd never in my life seen so much color in one room.

It reminded me of Isabelle's paintings in art class.

"Did you paint the flowers?" I asked.

She nodded. "Me and my mom. We like to paint things."

When we went down to the kitchen to have a snack I saw what she meant. The room was completely yellow. Checked curtains on the windows. Sunflower dish towels on a rack. And the table and chairs and cupboards were all painted bright yellow with dots and swirls and stripes of red and green giving them a lively happy look.

I must have been staring. Isabelle said as if she thought she ought to explain, "My mom wanted a sunny kitchen and this one was dark. So she decided to make it sunny herself."

I thought about that while Isabelle and I sat at the round yellow table and listened to her older brother's favorite awful radio station and ate a whole box of dough-nuts.

Was it really possible to turn something dark into something sunny with just a little bit of paint? Could just cutting your hair turn you into a completely new person?

Then I decided not to think about it.

I just sat in Isabelle's kitchen and felt sunny.

nineteen...

But something changed in the night.

In my dream I was on an escalator. Maybe in a department store or a mall or an airport. It was a really long escalator. And I was going down and right next to me on the other escalator people were going up. I kept seeing kids I knew like Melissa and Jen and Kristin and Eddie Gallagher and Alexander and I kept waving at them. Only no one waved back to me.

Mrs. McFeeley the school principal passed by and Mr. Jenkins the nice custodian but they didn't seem to see me either. And then my mother.

"Mom!" I called waving as hard as I could. I was so glad to see her.

She looked right past me as if she didn't know me.

I felt my hair in back where it was so short it barely touched my neck.

"It's me, Mom!" I cried. "Really. I don't look the same because I got my hair cut."

But she just kept going.

"Mom!"

Up and up and up smaller and smaller and finally out of sight. Into the ceiling or the sky.

I started crying and then I woke up and I was still crying. Holding on to my pillow and shaking all over like I was sick. And I ached in some deep-down place that I couldn't tell where it was.

I cried thinking of my mother getting smaller and smaller on that escalator until she disappeared. I should never have cut my hair I thought. I should always look the same so in case she comes back she will recognize me right away.

"Tell me where it hurts," said my mother's soft voice.

When I was little and got sick in the night she would always say that to me. She would sit on my bed and check my forehead to see if I had any fever and stroke my hair.

"All over," I said into my pillow.

Then I felt her hand stroking my hair. And just like

when I was little I felt myself getting quieter inside. My fear melting that awful ache beginning to fade away.

My mother would take care of me.

I opened my eyes and Lucy was there. With her wise eyes and smiling mouth and soft fur that looked almost white in the moonlight. She was stroking my hair with the gentlest of paws.

She kept smiling down at me and after a while I smiled back. Then strangely Lucy stood up on her hind legs.

"Shall we dance?" she said.

Suddenly music was in the room along with the moonlight.

I took Lucy's paw and we danced. Circling and twirling and gliding so smoothly all around the bed. And amazingly since I didn't know how to dance I never stumbled. My feet knew just what to do. It was as if the music was in my toes.

Just like Cassie I thought. This must be what it feels like being her.

We danced and danced in the white moonlight until finally I was so tired I fell into my bed still smiling.

As my eyes were closing I heard Lucy speak again.

"Good night," she said softly.

twenty...

My fame at school didn't last. By the end of the week everyone was talking about the ancient Egypt projects we had to do and Field Day that was coming up the last week of school and nobody looked at me anymore like I knew things. I was just ordinary again.

But being friends with Isabelle did last. We signed up to do our ancient Egypt project together so that meant we had to spend a lot of time deciding what it was going to be. We talked about it at lunch and after school at each other's houses.

Having Isabelle at my house broke up the quiet that was always there. I showed her Cassie's ten thousand beauty products and we did our eyes together in my boring all-beige bathroom.

"Oops!" I said. "Black eye again."

"Four black eyes," said Isabelle.

And we laughed looking at ourselves in the mirror.

I liked it better at her house. It was a small square light-green house that always seemed overflowing with stuff. Color and noise and people and animals. Her three brothers and their friends were outside playing baseball and inside playing music. The dog was barking and the cat was jumping up on things. A yellow bird named Tweetie was flying around landing every now and then in places that could give you a heart attack. And the phone was ringing all the time.

It was like my house turned inside out.

Isabelle sat at the yellow kitchen table with the pile of ancient Egypt books we'd taken out of the library and ignored it all.

"A pyramid would be fun," she said looking at a full-color picture of one. "We could take cardboard boxes and stack them up and then glue sand all over them."

Isabelle thought big. I could see that.

"Some of the boys are doing a pyramid," I told her. "Out of sugar cubes."

"Hmmm." She flipped some more pages of the book. "Then how about a mummy?"

Was she serious? What had I gotten myself into?

"Just kidding." Isabelle grinned. "But it would give Mrs. Deeley a fit, wouldn't it?"

I could picture it in my mind us carrying some life-size figure all wrapped in bandages into the classroom. That would definitely cause a stir with Mrs. Deeley.

"Maybe we need to think a little smaller," I suggested.

We sat there turning pages and I didn't really care if we found an idea for our ancient Egypt project or not. I just liked being in Isabelle's sunny yellow kitchen with the boys shouting in the backyard and the loud music upstairs and the bird sitting on top of the refrigerator.

"A mask!" said Isabelle suddenly. "Oh, this is perfect."

She held up a picture of a mask made out of real gold the way the Egyptians did for their dead kings. This king was wearing a strange striped headdress with a snake on top.

"How can we make a gold mask?" I asked.

"Easy," said Isabelle.

We worked in the basement which she called her artist's studio. It was filled with old bikes and soccer balls and hockey sticks and old furniture and piled-up cans of paint. She had every color you could think of.

The floor was like a painting by some modern artist. Covered with drips and splashes of all those paint colors.

You could have framed Isabelle's basement floor for a museum.

It took a few days to make our mask. First we had to build the face out of papier-mâché. Then when it was dry we sprayed it all over with gold paint. After that we added the details exactly like the picture in the book. Isabelle's mother's striped scarf and more paint and fake jewels glued on and a plastic snake borrowed from her little brother's reptile collection.

Isabelle kept checking the picture to make sure every detail was exactly right.

"Do you think those black beads are best for the eyes?" she would ask. "Or should we use marbles?"

I never worked this hard when I used to do school projects with Maggie. We would just make something easy and then go outside and ride our bikes. But I didn't mind. I liked being in Isabelle's basement as much as her kitchen. I liked getting paint slopped all over myself and adding my own drips to the floor. I liked making something where every little detail was exactly right.

Isabelle painted on the eyebrows with a tiny brush and it was finished.

We looked at our mask next to the mask in the book.

"Pretty good," said Isabelle.

"Actually great," I said.

It was amazing how much our mask looked like the real one even if the Egyptians' was gold and ours was just spray paint.

That was because of Isabelle. I could see now she was a real artist.

We were so excited we wanted to show someone. So we carefully carried the gold mask upstairs to the kitchen.

Six little boys in baseball hats were sitting around the table stuffing in cookies and spilling juice on themselves.

"Justin," said Isabelle to her brother. "Look what we made."

Justin looked up. "Hey," he said. "That's my snake. I didn't say you could have my snake."

"Is that supposed to be an alien?" asked another boy.

And laughing they picked up their bats and gloves and ran outside.

"They were impressed," said Isabelle.

She wiped off the sticky table so we could put down the mask.

The music from above got suddenly louder as her oldest brother came wandering downstairs with his radio on his shoulder.

"Hey Douglas!" shouted Isabelle. "Look at our Egyptian king."

Douglas didn't seem to notice. Nodding his head to his music he opened the refrigerator and took out a dish of something and then wandered back upstairs.

"He was overwhelmed," I said.

Isabelle started rummaging around in the cupboards for something to wrap the mask in to take it to school.

"That is absolutely wonderful!" said someone behind us.

"Mom." Isabelle turned around. "You're home early."

Isabelle's mother looked just like her. Or I guess the other way around. She had the same round face with the little smile that made it seem like something was funny most of the time. Her hair was red too but more of a dark maroony color and naturally it was cut and styled perfectly since she was in the beauty business.

"This is Morgan," Isabelle said. "We just finished our mask."

"Hi, Morgan." Isabelle's mother took my hand and squeezed it.

Her eyes were bright blue with smile crinkles around the edges. Looking at her I thought for just a tiny instant I was seeing my mother. She wasn't my mother or anything like her really but she was looking at me like a mother. And she touched me.

For another instant I thought I might cry but then Isabelle's mother was bending over the table looking at our mask.

"You two did a terrific job," she said. "Just look at those eyes. And the gorgeous headdress. That scarf looks better on him than it ever did on me. And Justin's snake worked out perfectly."

"See how close our mask is to the picture?" Isabelle opened the book again to show her.

Her mother nodded her head. "Remarkable," she said. "Mrs. Deeley is going to love it."

The idea of Mrs. Deeley loving anything made me smile. I looked at Isabelle and we both started to laugh.

Once we started we couldn't stop. In a minute Isabelle's mother joined in.

And we all three laughed and laughed standing around our beautiful mask on the yellow table in Isabelle's sunny kitchen.

twenty-one...

Mrs. Deeley did not love our mask. At least she didn't say so. But I think maybe she liked it pretty well since she gave us both an A and hung it in the best spot out in the hall when we had our display of ancient Egypt projects.

That is the most you can expect from Mrs. Deeley.

Then we had Field Day and we started taking things home and turning in our books and school was over.

It happened so fast.

Summer was here suddenly and I didn't know what to do.

I remember last summer I used to watch Ben in the mornings while my mother gave piano lessons. Mrs. Ellsworth was one of her students. She played so badly that Ben and I would have to go outside and even cover our ears sometimes. But my mother thought Mrs. Ellsworth was great because even though she was old and could barely walk she was still trying to learn something new. And she didn't notice that she played badly she was having such a good time. My mother loved Mrs. Ellsworth.

Then in the afternoons we would do something all together. Like making lemonade out of real lemons and mint from the garden. Or picking blackberries at the field behind the high school and then baking them into a pie. Or I would go with Maggie to the town pool. Sometimes Cassie even let me go to the pool with her but I had to act like I didn't know her if she saw her friends or especially any boys.

This year Cassie wasn't going to the pool. She was too busy with the summer theater group she was in and her job at the ice cream store downtown. And her boyfriend Sean who was giving her driving lessons in his red car with the silver wheels.

She was planning to take the driving test the day of her birthday September 9.

I couldn't go to the pool with Isabelle either. The minute school was out her family rented a camper and started driving cross-country to the Grand Canyon. She wouldn't be back for two weeks.

Even Alexander was busy. His father signed him up for day camp. Every morning a baby-size yellow school bus picked him up and didn't bring him back until late afternoon. Sometimes when he got home we played catch and he told me everything they had done that day at camp.

Alexander liked day camp. Except for making lanyards and clay pots on rainy days. They played baseball nearly every day. He had a new friend named Patrick. But the best thing was his mother was going to take him to a Yankee game in three weeks.

"I'm taking my glove with me," he told me. "Maybe I could catch a foul ball."

"I bet you will," I said.

After that we had to practice catching a hundred foul balls.

The thing I always noticed about summer was how slowed down everything felt. A day in July could seem like a week of the regular year. And this year it got hot right away as soon as school was out. When it was hot you didn't want to move fast but just take it easy in the hammock in the backyard with a library book and a cool drink. I had this idea that maybe clocks felt the same way. In hot weather they slowed themselves down and just took it easy.

It seemed that way to me while I waited for Isabelle to come home from the Grand Canyon.

My father kept asking if I'd like to take an art class or tennis lessons or maybe sign up to go to a sleep-away camp he'd heard about in Maine for the month of August.

But I said no.

What if my mother and Ben came back and I wasn't here?

She might come for the blackberries. She and Ben both loved picking blackberries. I have a little snapshot in my head of Ben going around with his tongue sticking out saying, "Look, I'm purple!"

I read a bunch of library books lying motionless in the hammock and wrote a letter to Maggie. But she didn't write back right away so I didn't have anyone else to write to. I thought about writing to my mother and Ben but where would I send it?

After a few days I got tired of lying in the hammock. I had finished my library books and my legs were twitching to do something. It was still too hot to move much though. Maybe Cassie would take me to the pool.

Just this once. It was her day off at the ice cream store and she didn't have a rehearsal till later.

"Cassie!" I called up the stairs.

"Is he here?" she called back.

Well that answered my question. She was going somewhere with Sean as always.

Cassie came bouncing down the stairs her perfect blond ponytail bobbing up and down.

"Oh. He's not here yet." She looked disappointed. "Why were you calling me?"

"I just thought," I said, "I mean if you weren't doing anything we could go to the pool."

"I can't," she said right away. "Sean is giving me another driving lesson. We just started parallel parking down by the train station. Guess how many times I did it yesterday."

"Twenty-five?"

"How did you know? But we could drop you off at the pool if you want."

I shook my head. "I guess not."

For the first time in a long time Cassie looked at me as if she was really seeing me.

"Why don't you call someone to go with?" she suggested. "What about your friend that you worked on your Egypt project with?"

"She's away," I said. "At the Grand Canyon."

"I'm sorry." Her voice really did sound sorry. "Maybe next week we could go, okay?"

"Okay."

"Oops, he's here." I saw a flash of red through the living room window. "Gotta go. Wish me luck!"

And away she flew out the front door.

The house was quiet again. So quiet it seemed as if I might be the only person alive in the world. I walked from the living room to the dining room where no one ever went anymore to the kitchen that used to be so neat when my mother was here. Fresh flowers on the table and all the dishes put away. Now dishes were piled in the sink and mail and library books stacked on the counter and shoes scattered on the floor. If she saw it today she'd say it looked like an earthquake hit.

She always used to say that. "Oh my! This house looks like an earthquake just hit it."

A messy kitchen drove her totally crazy.

I didn't want to look at it or clean it up so I went back to the living room.

I stood next to the piano. It was a black baby grand. A Steinway the best kind of piano to have. My mother loved that piano so much it was strange she didn't take it with her. But it is so big I guess she couldn't. It sat in the corner with its top closed down looking alone.

Our house used to be filled with piano sounds. I thought last summer all those wrong notes and too-loud chords would drive me out of my mind and I had to get away from them. Now though I kind of missed them. I even missed Mrs. Ellsworth playing badly.

When she left our house she was always smiling.

I lifted the top of the piano and dust flew out. Then I pulled out the bench and sat down.

It was a long time since I had played anything. My mother started giving me lessons when I was too young to reach the pedals. But I wasn't good at it like Cassie was until she decided she liked dancing better. I didn't want to practice and my mother would make me and set the kitchen timer for thirty minutes and we argued all the time. Finally she got tired of it and said I could decide whether I wanted to keep playing or not. But if I decided I wanted to I had to practice.

I decided not to.

Probably the piano was out of tune after all this time. I put my fingers on the white keys and played a chord. The sudden sound startled me.

I tried to think of anything I used to play. Something easy. "Twinkle, Twinkle, Little Star." That was the one the little kids usually started on. Amazingly as if they remembered my fingers picked it out. Then "Mary Had a Little Lamb." I'd heard that one a thousand times in this house.

The keys felt hard and slick and smooth. And the piano sounds filled up the empty space in the house so that for a minute it felt almost the way it used to. I wanted to keep going but after "Chopsticks" I couldn't think of any other music I knew by heart.

I opened up the piano bench and looked through the music piled inside. Near the top was a folder my mother kept of the music I was playing before I stopped. She used to give me a gold star when I played something all the way through without making a mistake. "Minuet in G." That one had four stars pasted on. "The Happy Farmer." Two stars. I always would make a mistake just at the end and miss my star. "Für Elise." That one was really hard. I never got a star on that.

I took out "Minuet in G" and put it up on the music stand and started playing.

It all came back to me how I used to sit there with the timer slowly ticking off my practice time and my mother in the kitchen making dinner. The good smells of chicken baking or spaghetti and meatballs making my stomach grumble.

Sometimes my mother would hear me playing the same wrong note over and over until she couldn't stand it. She would forget about dinner and sit down next to me on the piano bench.

"It's an F-sharp," she would say. "Let's mark it in red to remind you."

She would sit next to me close and warm.

If I kept on playing it might all come back. She would be sitting next to me again with her red pencil and the timer ticking and those good dinner smells coming from the kitchen.

I kept playing "Minuet in G" over and over filling the empty house with piano sounds.

twenty-two...

Finally Isabelle came back from the Grand Canyon. She was full of stories about the camper breaking down in the middle of nowhere and her little brother throwing up in a fast-food place and their whole family riding down into the canyon on mules. She was sure they would all fall off but they didn't and it was great.

She told me all this at my house on her first day home. The second day we went to the pool.

We lay on our backs on our beach towels in the grass. My towel was pink and hers was turquoise with bright yellow flowers all over it. It was hot again. Pretty soon we would have to go in the water.

"You should have seen the colors," Isabelle said in a

dreamy kind of voice. "Especially when the sun was coming up. We got up really early to see it."

She was still thinking about the Grand Canyon.

"I bet I could paint those colors."

It seemed like Isabelle wasn't quite back from her trip yet. I turned over. Through bright green spears of grass I could see the wading pool where the little kids were splashing around.

"That's my boat!"

A voice I knew. A red bathing suit with sailboats on it.

Ben I thought with a jolt.

I sat straight up and saw a boy with wrong-colored hair and a red bathing suit with stars.

Not Ben. Of course not.

Isabelle's brothers were all at the pool. Justin who she was supposed to be watching was with the same wild gang of boys he was always with doing cannonballs and splashing people at the deep end. Philip the eighth-grade one was practicing dives on the low board. Douglas the oldest was sitting up on one of the lifeguard chairs.

He looked different than when I saw him at her house. He had on a clean white Rec Department T-shirt and dark sunglasses and a silver whistle around his neck.

Tweet! He blew his whistle at the cannonballing boys.

Justin and his friends didn't even look up. One of them jumped in the water right next to two high school girls who started yelling at him.

Tweet! Tweeeeet!

"I think Justin's in trouble," I told Isabelle.

She sat up slowly blinking in the sun.

Douglas climbed down from his lifeguard chair. He walked to the deep end and crouched down at the edge of the pool. He said something to the cannonballing boys and right away they all got out of the water and sat down in the grass. The next minute they were running off to the snack bar.

Isabelle lay back down and closed her eyes.

I kept watching as Douglas climbed the ladder to the high diving board. For a few seconds he stood completely still on the end of the board with his arms straight out. Then he bounced high against the bright blue of the sky and did a perfect dive slicing the water with only the tiniest splash.

It was over so fast but it was so graceful like a ballet or something. It echoed in my head.

In another moment he was next to us pulling himself up by his arms out of the pool.

"Hey, Iz." Grinning he flicked water on Isabelle's back.

"Hey!" Isabelle sat up again.

Droplets of water glistened on his arms. His dark wet hair fell down on his forehead in just-right curls.

"Did I splash you? Oops, sorry." Still grinning Douglas climbed up on the lifeguard chair.

I felt like my breathing had stopped. A peculiar shaky sensation was in my knees. If I stood up I might fall over.

What was wrong with me? This was only Isabelle's brother. The one who always walked around with a radio glued to his ear.

I lay back down and closed my eyes waiting for those odd feelings to go away. But they didn't. Behind my eyes I still saw that wide grin and the water drops shimmering in the sun and those wet curls that went just exactly the way curls should go.

And the way he flew up into the sky and came back down.

"I'm getting hungry. Want to go to the snack bar?"

Isabelle's voice startled me.

"Oh. Sure."

My own voice sounded strange to me. I opened my eyes. Being careful not to look up at the lifeguard chair I dug my lunch money out of my beach bag and stood up.

"I think I'll have a hot dog," Isabelle decided as we walked toward the snack bar. "Or maybe grilled cheese.

Actually it doesn't matter as long as it's not peanut butter. We must have had a hundred peanut butter sandwiches in that camper in the last two weeks."

I didn't answer. I was noticing how bright blue the sky was and how the edges of things seemed clearer than they ever had before.

Was it my eyes or just something else strange about this strange day?

We sat down at a round white table under a green striped umbrella. Isabelle was still talking about peanut butter.

"You know what my brother called the camper? The peanut butter bus."

Brother.

"Which brother?" I asked.

"Oh," she said. "Douglas. He always thinks he's funny."

Douglas.

I said the name to myself over and over.

Douglas Douglas Douglas.

What a perfect name.

twenty-three...

Isabelle and I went to the pool every day except if it rained.

Every day we would put down our beach towels in the exact same spot in the grass near the lifeguard chair.

And every day while Isabelle was reading or lying with her eyes closed thinking about her Grand Canyon painting I was sneaking little peeks up at Douglas.

I noticed things about him.

He has big feet.

His hair when the sun is shining on it has red glints like somewhere inside is Isabelle and her mother's color.

His ears stick out a little but not too much.

He must get really hot sitting in that lifeguard chair. Because every little while he jumps down and does a quick dive into the pool and then climbs back up. His dives are like that first one. Neat as a knife cutting the water.

He is nice to the little kids. He talks to them and lets them hold his whistle but not blow it. Sometimes he even lets them sit up in the chair next to him for a minute. Just when another lifeguard comes on though. Not when he is on duty.

High school girls stand by the chair talking to him. Especially one named Amy Foster. Her brother Michael is in my class so I know who she is. She has long blond hair like Cassie's that I never have seen get wet. Probably she can't even swim. I never see her in the water. She stands around laughing at anything Douglas says.

I hate Amy Foster.

Douglas couldn't like her. He is such a good swimmer.

I wonder if he does though. I could ask Isabelle. But if I do I'll be sure to turn all red in the face and she will know I like him.

I don't know if I should tell her or not. Sometimes I really want to and it almost comes popping out of my mouth. But Isabelle is always saying bad things about him. She might give me her amazed look and say, "You *like* Douglas? How could you?" And then she would tell me about some terrible disgusting habit he had. And that would ruin everything.

Douglas does not know I'm alive. Well he knows Isabelle has a friend who she comes to the pool with. Probably he doesn't even know my name though.

Lying facedown on my beach towel with the sun burning hot on my back I would close my eyes and imagine all kinds of things that could happen.

I could see it like in a movie.

I am swimming laps and I get tired all of a sudden and I am at the deep end. I try to make it to the side of the pool but I'm all weak in the legs and I go under. I'm floundering around and then I see bubbles and feel someone grab my shoulder. Douglas is next to me lifting me up in his strong arms. Carrying me out of the pool.

That would never happen. I could always make it to the side of the pool.

Unless of course I was hit by a cannonballing boy and knocked unconscious. That's it. I am unconscious and have no idea what hit me. When I wake up I am lying flat in the grass and Douglas is looking down at me all worried and saying, "Morgan, are you all right?"

He knows my name.

Or else maybe I cut my foot on a piece of broken glass

that no one knew was hidden in the grass. This actually happened to a boy here last year. Douglas has to quick run and get the first-aid kit and wrap up my foot and maybe apply a tourniquet to stop the bleeding. I don't cry even though I can't stand the sight of blood. He is amazed at how brave I am.

None of these movies inside my head happened.

Mostly it was just quiet with Douglas sitting up in the lifeguard chair talking to Amy Foster and once in a while blowing his whistle at kids who were bothering people or swimming too close to the diving area.

Once or twice I thought he looked at me. Like when he got out of the pool and stood dripping water on Isabelle waiting for her to say "That's not funny, Douglas." But I wasn't sure.

If I could dive I bet he would notice me.

I mean really dive instead of what I did off the side of the pool to get in the water.

Everyone in Isabelle's family was a good diver. Isabelle herself did running dives and back dives off the low board and Philip was practicing a jackknife and Douglas did one from the high dive where he turned a complete somersault in the air before unwinding and shooting straight as an arrow into the water.

"Could you teach me to dive off the diving board?" I asked Isabelle.

"Sure," she said.

So I practiced standing with my toes curled around the end of the low board looking down at the water which looked far away. Then I did some bouncing and after a few more days I did an actual dive off the board.

It felt like I landed flat on my stomach. I hoped Douglas hadn't been watching. I looked over at the lifeguard chair and there was Amy Foster as usual and for once I was glad.

"That was great," Isabelle told me when I climbed out of the water. "Now you can start working on your back dive."

She liked to move right along.

The next few days I worked on my back dive which was scary because you are standing backwards and on tiptoe at the end of the board and you could slip and hit your head or something. Isabelle helped until I got the hang of it and then she started working on her own dives off the high board.

At first she was just jumping.

"This is fun!" she called as she climbed the ladder. "Morgan, you have to try it."

"No thanks," I said. I had my hands full with the low board.

She jumped over and over doing cannonballs with Philip or silly things like flapping her wings like a chicken in the air.

"I bet you an M&M you can't do this!" she or Philip would yell and then the other one would try to do it.

Isabelle and her brothers were always making bets like that.

"Come on, Morgan," she urged. "Just once. I promise you'll love it."

"I don't think so."

Isabelle was having such a good time she didn't stop even when the clock over the snack bar said five and all the mothers and little kids were packing up to go home.

I was ready to leave too feeling kind of waterlogged.

"Don't you want to try it once before we go?" Isabelle asked.

I shook my head.

"You could just climb the ladder and see what it's like. You don't have to jump."

Well maybe I could do that. I guessed. "Okay."

The steps to the high dive were really steep. I held tight to the green metal rail as I climbed.

Oh my. This was so high. Like being up in a tree.

Things down below looked really small like chairs and umbrellas and beach towels. Looking down on people's heads gave them a funny deformed shape. And the snack bar roof was red. I never knew that.

"Walk out on the board," said Isabelle from the bottom of the ladder. Only one person was allowed on the high dive at a time. "But don't look down."

There was nothing to hold on to. I inched out one step at a time carefully not looking down. This wasn't so bad. The board was just like the low one. Pretty wide with some special stuff under your feet so you wouldn't slip.

I could do this.

I got to the end of the board and stood still feeling a tiny bit of bounce under my toes.

"Bet you an M&M you won't jump!"

That was Philip. Without looking I could tell he had a big grin on his face.

"She doesn't have to," Isabelle said. "She's just getting used to the board."

"A nice fat red one!" Philip called.

A bet even for an M&M was serious. I would show him and Isabelle too I could do it.

I looked down.

Oh no that was a mistake. The pool looked bright blue and flat and hard in the slanting late-afternoon sun.

My knees started shaking. I couldn't jump into that. It would break me in pieces.

My whole body was shaking now. My head felt woozy like when you spin around in circles really fast and then have to sit down.

I would fall off.

I sat down on the end of the diving board.

"Morgan," called Isabelle's faraway voice. "Are you okay?"

"I got kind of dizzy," I said.

"Then come down."

"Okay."

But to come down I would have to turn around and then somehow get off the board. Walk or maybe crawl. I couldn't move.

I closed my eyes to try to stop the spinning.

"Morgan." A calm quiet voice behind me.

"Yes?"

"Take a deep breath. Breathe slowly in and out."

It was Douglas. The lifeguard come to save my life.

I did what he said. A few slow deep breaths and I felt a little quieter inside.

"Now try to turn toward me. Don't stand up. Just slowly swing your leg around."

I held tight to the board with both hands. Very carefully I edged myself around. Then slowly I lifted my leg over so I faced him.

"Good. Now grab my hand."

Douglas's hand was stretched out to me. He was smiling. His eyes were brown.

I reached out and he had me strong and steady. Slowly he pulled me up and held on to my shoulder and walked me off the diving board.

My knees were still shaking when I reached the ground.

"Are you okay?" Isabelle looked worried.

I felt cold besides being all shaky but I nodded. "Sure."

A bunch of boys were standing around the diving area looking up at Douglas with big eyes.

"Did you save her?" asked one of Justin's friends.

"Well kind of," said Douglas. He walked back to the lifeguard chair with the bunch of boys following him.

"Let's go home," I said to Isabelle.

We gathered up our stuff and she walked me home. It wasn't until we got to my street that my knees felt normal again.

"Don't worry about it," Isabelle said. "You'll go off the high dive some other time."

"Or not," I answered. "I don't even like M&Ms that much."

"Right. No pressure."

I went up to my room and sat on my bed with my quilt wrapped around my shoulders and after a few minutes I finally felt warm.

He knows my name I thought. I touched his hand.

twenty-four...

It is awful having a secret and no one to tell it to. No one at all that I could say Douglas's name to.

For about one minute I thought of telling Cassie. But she was so far away with her driving lessons and theater workshop and her boyfriend Sean who she went out with almost every night. She would probably just look at me blankly and go on filing her nails. Or I could write to Maggie. But she seems so far away now too and how could I put it down in writing without sounding stupid? I really wanted to tell Isabelle but I was afraid of what she might say.

So I said his name to myself about a hundred times a day. And I thought of reasons to say it out loud while Isabelle and I were lying side by side on our beach towels every day at the pool. Not too often though so she wouldn't get suspicious.

"So what colleges did you say Douglas was thinking about going to after he graduates?"

"He doesn't know yet. He is so lazy he might not even get into college."

"Really? He seems pretty smart."

Very long pause.

"Do you think Douglas likes that girl Amy who is always hanging around the lifeguard chair?"

"I don't think so. He says she is a pain. But he keeps talking to her so I don't know."

"She is a total pain. All she does is comb her hair and go look at herself in the mirror in the girls' bathroom. I bet she hasn't been in the water once this summer."

That conversation gave me an idea. When Amy Foster wasn't in the girls' bathroom or hanging around Douglas she was sitting with her friend in the grass right by the edge of the pool. Next to the diving area.

Just one time she needed to get soaked.

So while I was practicing my dives off the low board and looking to see if Douglas was watching because I thought I was getting a little better I would splash as much as I could swimming back to the ladder. I did the butterfly which was my splashiest stroke.

Pretending of course that I was totally concentrating on my swimming. I didn't mean to get anyone wet.

It kind of worked. Once or twice out of the corner of my eye I saw Amy and her friend move their towels back. Frowning like they felt a few drops.

That was a start. But it wasn't enough.

Douglas needed to see that long blond hair of hers hanging down all limp and wet. Something mean in me wanted that.

The way it happened was a total accident. Really.

Isabelle had been giving me some pointers that day on my back dive. And finally I thought I was starting to get the hang of it. I dove in after her and was butterflying back to the ladder. I didn't see Justin and his friends playing one of their silly tag games in the water. But by mistake I must have splashed them.

"Hey!" said Justin.

Of course he splashed me.

Naturally I splashed him back.

Right away his friends joined in. So did Isabelle.

All of a sudden everyone was splashing everyone and we were all laughing and the boys were yelling, "Water fight!"

"You kids stop that!"

Through a haze of water drops I saw legs jumping

around at the edge of the pool. And scowling faces. And someone shaking their long limp sopping-wet hair.

Was she ever mad! Amy Foster looked like she could spit nickels as my grandmother used to say.

I wished I could take a picture of that moment to remember it forever.

Tweet! Tweeeet! Tweeeeet!

Douglas was standing up in his lifeguard chair blowing on his silver whistle.

"Cut it out, you guys!" he yelled. "No water fights, you know that. Justin! Morgan! Out of the pool!"

His face was red. He looked really angry. And he was yelling at me. He knew my name for sure.

That didn't seem so great right now.

Isabelle and I and Justin and all his friends climbed out of the pool with everybody staring at us. I didn't look up at the lifeguard chair but just walked over to my towel and lay down next to Isabelle.

I tried to figure out if this was a good moment or an awful one.

Amy Foster had disappeared. Probably to the girls' bathroom to try to fix her hair. That could take a long time. Maybe she would never come out.

But Douglas had yelled at me.

Good and awful at the same time I decided. Like sweet and sour.

Lying there with my eyes closed I could still see Amy Foster's drowned-rat hair and her angry face.

And I had to smile.

If only I'd had my camera to take her picture.

twenty-five...

A couple of days later I brought my camera to the pool. I hadn't felt like taking pictures for a long time. Not since Halloween right before my mother and Ben left. I took a bunch of pictures then of Ben in his costume that my mother made out of a cardboard box and paper plates before I took him out trick-or-treating.

"Do you know what I am?" he asked at every house.

"Let me see," they would say pretending to think it over. "Could you be a car?"

"Vrrrooom!" He would race his engine. "I'm a racing car."

Ben looked so cute in his car costume. And the pictures I took that day came out great.

Pictures of Ben always came out great.

Now Isabelle and I had a plan. We were going to photograph each other's dives so we could see how well we were doing. Then we would know what we still had to work on.

We started at the high dive.

After what had happened I still couldn't bring myself to climb that ladder again. Every time I thought about it I remembered what it felt like standing at the end of the diving board looking down. But Isabelle never gave it a thought. She had gone quickly from just jumping to diving and now was even thinking of trying a somersault.

"Ready?" she called down to me.

"Ready."

She leaned out and did her plain straight dive and I snapped a picture just as she hit the water. At least I thought I did.

"That was a good one," I told her when she came out. "Hardly any splash."

I moved to the other side of the board to take one from a different angle.

In the viewfinder I could see the lifeguard chair in the background. Not so far away either. While I was taking pictures of Isabelle maybe I could get one of Douglas too.

That would be so cool.

So every time I lined up a picture I made sure Douglas was in it somewhere. Mostly kind of tiny in the background sitting up in his chair. But then he came down and stood talking to some little kids and was bigger. And once he walked over near the diving board.

I saw it happening and my hand shook holding the camera. Isabelle was just climbing the ladder not even on the board yet. But I didn't wait. I squeezed the shutter.

Probably it will come out all blurry since my hand was shaking. And I can never show Isabelle that picture that doesn't have her in it just Douglas. I will have to hide it.

But I will have it.

"Now I'll take some of you," said Isabelle.

I gave her the camera and went to the low board and did some front dives that weren't as good as usual because I knew she was taking pictures of them.

Then I tried my back dive.

The first one was awful. I slipped and kind of fell sideways into the water.

"I hope you didn't take that one," I said as I climbed out.

She shook her head.

I did a couple more lopsided ones.

"Well, at least you can see what you need to work on," said Isabelle.

Finally I did one that felt good. When my head popped out of the water Isabelle was smiling.

"Fantastic!" she said. "I think I got it too. That will be a great one to show your mom."

I just looked at her.

"Oh." Isabelle's mouth made a sound like a balloon with its air leaking out. Her face sagged. "I'm sorry," she said. "I don't know why I said that."

"That's okay," I mumbled.

But I was walking away from her. Past the lifeguard chair. Past my towel with all my stuff piled around it. Past the wading pool with the laughing little kids in their bright bathing suits. Red with sailboats or stars.

"Wait!" called Isabelle behind me. "Morgan, please wait!"

Finally she caught up to me near the snack bar.

"I'm sorry," she said again. "It's the most awful thing that your mother died."

twenty-six...

She didn't die. She left.

That was what I was screaming out loud or maybe not maybe just inside my head that felt like it was bursting as I ran past the snack bar with the smell of hot dogs and french fries and was that Amy Foster sitting there with her friend what's-her-name but it didn't matter I didn't care and then out the gate onto the sidewalk with cars flashing by and houses sitting quietly in the hot sun with bright dots of flowers in the yards and a pointy-eared black dog on a chain barking furiously at me running by.

Isabelle wasn't behind me anymore. I knew it without looking. But I kept running until I got to my house but I didn't want to be there either all empty I knew so I kept going. Past Alexander's house and the Thompsons' and the redbrick house where the new people just moved in and then on to the next block. Slowing down now because of the pain in my side and my breath that came in ragged gasps. Slowing down to a walk.

And finally stopping.

I saw I was across the street from my old school. The one I went to from kindergarten to third grade.

It was all shut down like it was sleeping.

I needed to sit down. My legs were wobbly and my head felt light as if it might leave my body and fly away.

There were the swings with the different color seats just like they used to be. Red and blue and yellow and green. And the slide and seesaw and the climbing bars that had seemed so high.

I crossed the street and sat shaking down on the red swing that was always my favorite. The metal chains squeaked as I swayed back and forth scuffing my sandals in the dirt.

I remembered that sound. I used to run to these swings at recess trying to be the first to get one so I could pump my legs harder and harder feeling myself going higher and higher looking up into the trees. Thinking my toes might scrape the sky. Thinking maybe if I pumped hard enough I might even fly.

When I was little my mother used to push me on these swings.

My mother.

My chest felt pinched. I couldn't breathe.

I saw her and Ben at the airport. Ben's nose squashed against the window staring out at his airplane. I saw them getting on the plane waving good-bye. Ben's smiling bear Fred peeking out of his backpack the last thing I saw.

"Take good care of Dad," my mother whispered.

"Have fun on your airplane!" I called to Ben.

They never got off that plane. It fell out of the sky.

How could that possibly be?

Things were rushing at me now. Bits and pieces of things I remembered. The phone ringing and Aunt Susan's voice sounding strange and asking to talk to my father not saying anything to me like she usually did. The TV on all the time with Special Bulletins and serious-looking announcers talking in concerned voices about the crash of Flight 109 and that was their flight number I remembered. And Cassie's face white as I'd never seen it before coming in the door.

Waiting and waiting through that long night. My father drinking cup after cup of coffee in the kitchen while the phone kept ringing. And then him holding on to the telephone repeating words someone was saying to him and slowly sinking down into a chair.

"No survivors."

It couldn't be.

My mother who loved us and never did anything wrong in her whole life. She was nice to everyone. Everyone said so. Just look now nice she was to that little girl Claudia at her first recital and to old Mrs. Ellsworth too. And she played the piano so beautifully it could about make you cry. And a little boy so excited about his first airplane ride. How could they be taken away?

More flashes of scenes rushed at me like a movie played at the wrong speed.

My two great-aunts from far away wearing black dresses and Mrs. Ellsworth bent over her cane and my little cousin Adam looking grown-up in a jacket and tie and hugs and "So sorry" from people in dark suits and dresses and too much perfume I couldn't remember their names and flowers too many flowers and the minister saying words I couldn't listen to because if I did I would break into a thousand pieces right there in the church.

It rained that day of the memorial service. A cold gray drizzle the one thing that felt exactly right. I don't think I could have stood it if the sun had been shining.

The organ played. Some quiet music that I had heard before. Maybe she used to play it on the piano I don't know.

My father held both our hands Cassie's and mine very tight. I wanted him to keep doing that forever.

It was just a dream it didn't really happen. She didn't die. She left. My mother and Ben ran away and never came back.

No they didn't this was real.

"No survivors," said my father's voice.

I couldn't stand my thoughts. I had to get away from them.

I twisted the chains of the swing around and around until they were wound up tight as they could be and then I let them go and spun around so fast I was dizzy.

When I was little I used to like doing that. But now I felt sick.

The playground was spinning and my head was pounding and my stomach churning so I thought for sure I was going to throw up.

I stood up and ran all the way home.

twenty-seven...

I lay in bed for three days. Cassie brought me toast on a tray in the mornings before she went to her rehearsal. My father took my temperature and wanted to take me to the doctor but I said no.

"It's just a little flu," I told him. "I'll be all right."

"Well, you don't have a fever," he said. He brought me chicken soup from the deli downtown when he came home.

Isabelle called and I told her I was sick. I don't know if she believed me.

I lay in bed under my sunbonnet-girl quilt and didn't answer the telephone and read a little of a mystery book but couldn't remember what I read and slept and woke up and nibbled a little cold toast.

Lucy did not come.

I wanted her to come but she didn't.

I got out of bed and walked around the house in my pajamas and turned on the TV and saw two women with blond hair yelling at each other and turned off the TV and looked out the window at Alexander's house empty like mine and got back in bed.

I felt like I was waiting for something but I didn't know what it was.

Lucy. Where are you? I need you to come now.

The dream came that night.

I was in an airplane looking out the window. Clouds stretched out as far as I could see soft and white and fluffy like whipped cream in a bowl. Soft but firm too like you could step off the wing of the plane and take a walk on those clouds. As I kept looking they seemed to change. Now the white was more blue-white like snow and in the distance were snow-covered mountains and maybe a sea. But it didn't look cold. I thought if I stepped down off the wing and took a walk I might meet a polar bear or a seal or maybe a little line of penguins dressed in their black-and-white suits.

It would be fun. I wanted to do it but I was a little scared too and then just ahead I saw my mother and Ben.

They were standing on a cloud. They saw me and

Ben smiled his great big bouncing smile and waved. I waved back. The airplane seemed to be slowing down and I was trying to open the window so I could climb out. I needed to get to them and hold on to them so they wouldn't leave.

But the window wouldn't open. I beat on it trying to break it but it wouldn't break.

My mother was beckoning me to come but I couldn't get through that glass it was so hard and now the airplane was speeding up again and they were past.

I looked back and saw them. My mother and Ben hand in hand skipping away across the snowy clouds.

I woke up.

My heart was pounding beating much too fast and loud in my ears. My pajama top was damp and I felt hot like I did have a fever after all. There was no air in my room.

I had to get some air.

I kicked off my quilt and got out of bed. I walked past my father's and Cassie's closed doors and down the stairs but there was no air there either so I opened the front door.

It must have been midnight or even later. The sky was black with no moon or stars. No lights were on in any of the houses except one dim one upstairs in the Steins' house across the street.

I sat down on the steps and breathed in air cooler now and smelling faintly of roses.

The air felt heavy. My father would say a storm was coming before morning.

After a few minutes I stood up and started walking. Past dark sleeping houses and dull glints of cars in driveways and hunched bushes that would have seemed spooky once but not tonight. Around the corner and a dog barking and a TV set flickering inside someone's family room so I wasn't the only one awake in the world and then down another block around another corner to the pool.

The gate was closed and locked with a padlock. But I climbed over it my feet fitting into the diamond-shaped spaces between the wires no problem.

The pool at night looked strange. The metal bones of chairs and umbrellas clustered around a long dark flat rectangle that glittered from the one bright white light in the parking lot. The high dive like an upside-down L at one end and the wading pool a round dot at the other. What is this place? I could imagine one space visitor asking another.

It was so quiet. I walked in the peculiar stillness along the edge of the pool to the high dive and started climbing the ladder. Up and up into the darkness holding on to the rail. I knew where I was stepping. I had been here before.

At the top I stopped.

My head could be touching the sky. The water below could be a hundred feet deep or two feet it was so black you couldn't tell.

A little breeze moved my pajamas lightly brushing my skin.

I let go of the rail and took a step forward. Then another feeling the rough-smooth diving board under my feet.

I wasn't dizzy. Very slowly one step at a time I kept going until I got to the end of the board.

What was I doing here? Why had I come?

I didn't look down. That would be the worst thing.

I could do this. I was going to do it. It was important. Why?

No one was betting me an M&M that I couldn't.

My mother and Ben were waving at me from the clouds. They were up above me watching somewhere in the dark sky.

No they weren't. They had fallen out of the sky. That was true and was going to stay true.

I had to do this.

I curled my toes around the end of the diving board

holding on. I felt the board tremble beneath me or maybe that was my knees trembling.

I took a deep breath filling my lungs full as they could be and jumped.

Down and down and down I fell like a stone. The water exploded and I kept falling. Down and down and down into a deep black hole. Down a hundred feet or maybe forever and time stood still black as the sky I had fallen out of.

It was peaceful there in the darkness. Quiet and peaceful. And there was no way to get back up it was much too far and I had no more breath no more strength in my arms or legs no more

nothing.

Then all at once something was holding me lifting me up. Gripping me under the armpits and saying, "Come on, Morgan. Up, up. You can do this. You can."

Lucy.

Lucy was there. She had me and I couldn't sink.

"Just a little farther," she was whispering in my ear. "It's all right. I am here."

My lungs were bursting. Lucy held me and I reached up straining out of that blackness my arms aching bubbles in my ears at last at last gasping in air.

I breathed. Choking out water and taking in air. A

circle of shimmering ripples spreading out around me on the dark surface of the pool.

Lucy was there still. Her large head next to mine. Her wet fur fanned out like a rug. I held on to it my fingers wrapped in it and she took us to the ladder and we climbed out.

I collapsed on the grass just breathing and waiting for strength to return to my arms and legs if it ever would.

Lucy shook herself water drops flying like a shower of tears.

She curled herself into a circle next to me and I rested against her. She was big and warm and safe and I wanted her never to leave me.

Her eyes glowed yellow in the dark.

"Are you all right?" she asked after a while.

"Yes," I answered.

"You know I will always be here."

Her voice was husky soft. Not growlly like it always had been before. Was that Lucy's voice or my mother's?

I looked up into the sky. Now I could make out faint pinpoints of faraway stars.

"Always," said Lucy.

twenty-eight...

I needed to talk to Isabelle but I didn't know what to say.
I was eating a bowl of cereal and staring at the phone
when it rang.

"Hey," she said. "How are you feeling?"

"Better," I said.

"Do you want to go to the pool today?"

I couldn't. Not yet.

"Not today," I said. "Maybe tomorrow."

"Okay."

A pause.

"Uh—Isabelle?" I began.

"Yeah?"

"I can't talk about my mom right now."

"Sure," she said right away. "That's okay, no problem."

I couldn't think of anything else to say. I was going to hang up when Isabelle said, "Maybe you could paint it."

"What?"

"How you feel, I mean. About your mom."

"Oh. Well. Maybe."

"I'll call you tomorrow, okay?"

"Okay."

I hung up the phone and finished my soggy cereal thinking about what Isabelle had said.

I could paint it.

Could I? Could I take paint the way she did and make it flow over the paper and say something about my mother and Ben too and make myself feel some way better?

No. I didn't think so. I wasn't an artist like Isabelle.

I walked around the house looking at things and seeing my mother in them like the kettle on the stove she was always heating up for her afternoon cup of tea. Her favorite blue mug with the yellow sunflowers. She loved blue and she loved flowers. My grandmother's old clock with the strawberries painted on the glass that my mother wound up every morning but now no one did. The dining room curtains that she made too short and had to take apart and start over. She didn't like sewing the way she liked cooking.

Her piano.

Most of all that was my mother.

I ran my hand over its smooth black top and then sat down on the hard bench looking at the keys. This was where she sat every day. Her feet resting on the pedals and hands curved lightly over the keys. Her fingers would fly over those keys so easily so smoothly. Notes would come pouring out tinkling like water or little bells or sometimes crashing like thunder or other times so quiet it was nearly no sound at all. It seemed so easy the way she played.

She loved Bach and Mozart.

Mozart made her smile and Bach made her cry. Not with sadness she said. With joy that there could be such beauty in the world.

I thought about the recitals she had. The ones for the little kids especially. She always had them at our house because she said it was hard enough to play for other people without having to do it in a strange place. And she would be busy for a whole week getting ready. Cleaning and borrowing extra chairs and baking cookies and printing up a program. By the day before she'd be tired and cranky. But the day of the recital when the little kids came looking scared she would be all calm and smiling. Hugging each one making them feel like this recital thing was no big deal just fun and in a minute they would all have cookies.

I think that is what they remembered most: the cookies. She made them in funny shapes like elephants and chickens and airplanes and musical notes. One year she even made pianos with white and chocolate frosting for the keys.

The little kids had fun at her recitals. And if anyone got mixed up while they were playing and looked like they were going to cry my mother helped them find their place so they could start over.

Once I remember a little girl named Claudia started over three times. She kept getting lost and finally she just stopped playing. She sat there and it was quiet in the room and tears were rolling down her cheeks so she couldn't even see the music. My mother came and sat down next to her and said, "Let's play our duet."

They played "Twinkle, Twinkle, Little Star" and everyone clapped really loud and Claudia took a bow smiling the biggest smile I ever saw.

I had to smile myself remembering that.

So many things about my mother I remembered.

Playing cards at the kitchen table when I was sick.

She didn't really like card games and that was the only time she would play with me just when I was sick. But once we got started we would play and play. Go Fish and Crazy Eights and Double Solitaire. Slapping down the cards and arguing and laughing until she would beg for us to quit because I was beating her so badly.

Ice-skating on the pond that time when she was trying to teach me and she tripped over her own skates and fell. She looked so surprised lying there. The mother on the ground and the child looking down not the way it was supposed to be.

"Are you all right, Mommy?" I asked all worried and she smiled and said, "Of course I am."

She wasn't though. It turned out she had sprained her ankle and it was weak after that so she never could really skate much again.

My mother in the garden fussing over her tomatoes. Fertilizing and watering and tying them up on poles with strips of old sheets. She talked to them too. I heard her though she never would admit it.

"There now," she would say. "You'll like that."

Patting them on the head like one of her students.

Her tomatoes grew tall and blossomed and little green fruits popped out and turned into big green fruits and finally red ripe ones the biggest sweetest juiciest tomatoes. Sometimes my father measured them and told her she had a prizewinner there. "Blue ribbon at the county fair," he would say. And her tomatoes kept on coming right up to frost. Some years we had tomatoes on Thanksgiving Day.

I could still taste them. Much better than the ones from the farm stand.

I missed those tomatoes.

I missed her.

And Ben too. My funny little brother. His round face with the fringe of sand-colored hair hanging over his eyes. His car collection arranged all over the couch so you couldn't sit down because you'd wreck his racetrack. His bouncy little-boy walk. His questions that went on and on until you wanted to scream but you didn't because you knew he really wanted to know. The way he slept with Fred the bear's head next to his on the pillow.

For his third birthday Ben had a cake with a lawn mower on top. That was before cars when he loved lawn mowers more than anything.

It hurt to remember. I felt an ache that started in my head and spread out all over my body. Even my toes hurt. And my skin and my eyeballs.

A word popped into my mind. *Mourning.* That must be what was happening to me.

I could change my name from Morgan to Mourning.

My fingers pressed down on the piano keys. Played a scale I remembered from a long time ago.

If only I had worked harder I could have played the piano. Maybe even as well as my mother someday. Well probably not. But I knew she wanted me to. I knew that even when I was too small to reach the pedals. She wanted me to love the piano as much as she did and I wouldn't do it.

Why wouldn't I?

I'm sorry Mom. So sorry.

"Minuet in G" was still sitting on the piano staring at me with its four shiny gold stars.

All right. I would play it for her now.

I played it all the way through. But it wasn't right. I could hear her voice inside my head telling me to watch for the F-sharp and speed up here and softer there. This is Bach she would always remind me. A minuet is a dance. Keep up the tempo but be sure it is smooth and even.

I played it over and over. Ten times or more.

After a while my fingers seemed to make a connection between the notes on the page and the sounds in my ears. I could feel the way a minuet should be like a dance and almost feel what the composer must have felt when he wrote it and feel how my mother felt the music and feel what I felt about my mother.

And finally I played "Minuet in G" by Bach.

When I played the last note I started to cry. Tears rolled down my cheeks until I couldn't see the music anymore and I put my head down on my mother's piano and just cried.

twenty-nine...

Alexander came home from his Yankee game with a baseball.

A real Yankee baseball. I couldn't believe it. He actually caught one.

"I *almost* caught it," he told me. "I saw it coming and I stood up and reached as high as I could with my glove."

He stood on his toes and showed me how high he reached.

"But it was too high. But then the man behind us caught it and gave it to me because he already has about ten baseballs at home. He goes to a lot of games."

"That was really nice," I said. "Can I see it?"

"Okay. But be careful. Don't drop it." He handed the ball to me.

The real Yankee baseball looked brand-new except for a tiny scuff you could hardly see on one side.

"I had three hot dogs and two sodas and an ice cream," Alexander said. "And you know what?"

"What?"

"I didn't get sick. My mom said I would but I didn't."

"You fooled her," I said.

Alexander nodded. "And you know what else?"

"What?"

"She bought me a yearbook with all the Yankee players in it and a pennant for my wall. My dad's going to put it up over my bed tonight. And this Yankee shirt."

Alexander's Yankee shirt looked like it would fit his dad. It hung down over his shorts like a dress.

"Cool shirt," I said.

"It was the best one they had but they didn't have my size but I got it anyway. My mom says I'll grow into it."

In about ten years I was thinking but I didn't say it.

"Sure you will. How was the game?"

"Good. You can see it on TV better than there. Yankee Stadium is really big and the players look far away so you can't even see their faces. I saw Babe Ruth's number on the left-field wall. He was number three and no one can ever have that number again."

"Did the Yankees win?"

Alexander nodded. "Six to five. They got four home runs. You should have seen this one the catcher hit to center field. It was hit a mile, the man behind us said."

"You were lucky to see so many homers."

I should have known what he would say next.

His face screwed up in a frown. "I've got to practice hitting home runs. Would you pitch to me?"

"Okay."

Alexander put his real Yankee baseball carefully on the doormat by the back door and got his red plastic bat and ball.

He tapped the bat on the piece of board that was home plate and looked at me with a terrible scowl.

That must be how the Yankee players did it on TV.

I pitched the ball. He took a gigantic swing and missed.

"Hey, Alexander," I said. "How come you're holding the bat that way?"

He had it up around his ears.

"That's how the catcher held it when he hit his homer," he explained.

I threw another one.

Alexander took another huge swing and missed.

I kept throwing and Alexander kept missing. Except a couple of times when he hit a little pop-up that would have been a foul ball. He kept trying though. Finally he swung so hard he turned himself completely around and sat down in the grass.

Tears were in his eyes when he stood up.

"Let's take a break," I suggested.

We sat down on his steps.

"You know Babe Ruth struck out a lot too," I told him.

"I know." Alexander nodded. "Over a thousand times."

"So you just have to keep working on it."

His face brightened a little. "I forgot to tell you. My mom said she would take me to another game. Maybe even the playoffs or the World Series if the Yankees keep winning."

"That would be fantastic," I said. "You have a good mom."

"Yeah," said Alexander. "She's nice."

I took a long slow deep breath.

"I had a good mom too," I said.

"Did she take you to baseball games?" Alexander asked.

"No."

I looked down at my sandals with little pieces of grass stuck all over them. Alexander's dad must have just cut it.

"But she did a lot of other stuff," I said. "A lot of really good stuff."

thirty...

I went back to the pool.

The summer went on like it had been. I lay on my towel and snuck peeks at Douglas and practiced my dives with Isabelle and got some better.

Isabelle got really good. She did somersaults now and sometimes she had her timing down just exactly right and went into the water straight. Douglas said if she kept it up she could be on the swim team when she got to high school.

Amy Foster and her friend started hanging out at the snack bar. Either she was afraid of getting her hair wet again or she had a new crush. I think she liked the skinny dark-haired guy named Mark who cooked the hot dogs and hamburgers on the grill. Whenever Isabelle and I went over there she was eating a hot dog.

The pictures I took of Douglas and our dives came out pretty well. The close-up one of him was blurry just like I thought but I keep it in the drawer of my night table under my tissue box anyway.

At home when no one was around I practiced the piano. "Minuet in G" and some other harder pieces that were in my folder. I didn't know why I was doing it exactly. Maybe I was trying to make up for not practicing before when my mother wanted me to. Or maybe it was because touching the piano keys she had touched so often seemed almost like touching her. If I stopped she would be gone a little more.

One afternoon my father came home from work earlier than usual. I was playing something loud and didn't hear him walk in. I don't know how long he was standing in the doorway before I looked up.

His shoulders were slumped in his suit. His eyes looked shiny.

I stopped playing not sure what to say.

"For a minute," he said in a hoarse voice, "I thought it was your mother playing."

"I'm sorry," I said.

"No." He shook his head like he was coming out of a dream. "Don't be sorry. Keep on playing. She would like that."

I couldn't though. I could see pain in his face and in the slow way he walked upstairs. In another few minutes he would be pounding away in his workshop in the basement.

I couldn't help my father and he couldn't help me. That was clear. I didn't know why but it was true.

Maybe after a long time he would pound away the pain.

Maybe I would too on the piano keys.

Maybe.

And what about Cassie? Would she dance it away? Or run so fast and far she would leave it all behind?

Cassie surprised me a few days later. She knocked on my bedroom door and asked if I'd like to go to the pool with her.

I opened the door still in my pajamas.

"You're not having a driving lesson?"

Amazingly she was still in her pajamas too. Usually she would be out the door by now.

She shook her head.

"Sean's car broke down yesterday. His brother is helping him put in a new something-or-other today."

I thought about it. Strange but I didn't really want to go to the pool with Cassie anymore. The pool was Isabelle now and Douglas and the little cannonballing boys and even Amy Foster.

Cassie didn't fit there.

"I—I wasn't going to the pool today." I searched my mind for a reason. And suddenly found one. "I was just thinking that the blackberries behind the high school must be ripe. Want to go pick some?"

Cassie looked at me. Slowly she nodded. "Sure."

We dressed the way we always used to in our oldest grubbiest clothes. Jeans and our worst sneakers and the special blackberry-picking shirts my mother insisted we wear. Worn-out too-big shirts of my father's that covered us practically from head to toe so we wouldn't get pricked by those sharp blackberry thorns. My white shirt still had faint purple splashes from last summer. I'd grown into it a little since then I noticed. I only had to roll up the sleeves three times.

I looked around until I found the plastic buckets we always carried. Then Cassie and I walked over to the high school.

We didn't talk much. I couldn't think of what to say. Cassie seemed like she'd gone even farther away since the beginning of the summer.

The blackberries were definitely ripe. Big and plump and shiny purple-black. And there were so many of them.

"Enough for a pie," I said.

"At least," answered Cassie. "Maybe two."

Only once that I could remember had we ever gotten enough berries for two pies. This was a good year.

We started picking.

"Remember the rules," I reminded her. "Four for one."

"Right."

You had to put four berries in your bucket for every one you ate. Well except for Ben. Even though he could count up to twenty perfectly well he seemed to forget how when he picked blackberries. For him it was three for one or sometimes even two for one.

He never got sick though. He just slowly turned purple all over.

I popped a berry into my mouth. It burst into sweet juiciness that was the taste of summer.

"Mmm, yum," I said.

Then four for the bucket and another for me.

In no time the sun was burning hot on my back. I could feel the sweat running down my neck on account of wearing my father's shirt. This was always the time I would start complaining about why we hadn't worn our bathing suits instead.

I reached into a bush and found five ripe berries all in a clump. Four for the bucket and one for me. I looked down at the warm berry bleeding purple onto my palm. I had never noticed before that a blackberry wasn't just one round ball like a blueberry but a bunch of tiny balls kind of glued together.

How strange. I wanted to show Cassie but she had moved away to another bush.

Moved away. My sister kept moving away.

Her head was turned so all I could see was her ponytail neat as always. And the smooth curve of her cheek. Smooth. Her face was so smooth and still it scared me. And she wasn't even doing four for one just dropping all her berries into her bucket.

"Cassie!" I said suddenly sticking out my tongue. "Am I purple yet?"

She turned and looked at me. Her eyes had gone funny.

"Ben," she said like a sigh.

Then she dropped her bucket and started crying.

I could see Ben in my mind plain as could be in my father's short-sleeved shirt that was long sleeves for him all dotted purple.

"I know," I said and I was crying too.

We moved toward each other and sat down in the grass both of us crying and shaking.

She never touched me Cassie didn't. Not for years. But now she did. I had my head bent over my knees and after a while she put her hand on my shoulder the way my mother would.

"Hey," she said.

That made me cry more. I cried until finally I wound down like one of those metal toys with the key in its side I had when I was small. A clown I think it was. My head ached and I felt hollow inside.

Cassie's eyes were red like mine must have been. Long strands of hair stuck out from her ponytail.

That wasn't like Cassie. She didn't reach up to tuck them in either.

"Do you think we'll ever forget?" I asked.

Cassie shook her head. "I don't know," she said. "I try to go on with my life and keep busy and it works for a while but not really. Because eventually you get so tired you have to stop and there it is waiting for you."

"I dream about them a lot," I said. "Do you?"

"All the time."

That surprised me. Behind our two closed doors we could be dreaming the same dreams.

"Maybe," I said trying out a thought. "Maybe we shouldn't forget. Maybe we need to remember things. Even though it's hard and hurts so much."

"Maybe," said Cassie.

We were quiet again for a few minutes.

Then Cassie said, "Remember how Ben used to ask so many questions? And one time Mom said he'd have to be quiet now because she was all out of answers. And Ben was quiet for about one minute and then he asked, 'Did you get some more answers yet?'"

I felt myself almost smiling. That was a good thing to remember.

"He was such a funny little kid," I said. "Remember all the stuff he was always bringing in from the yard? Caterpillars and moss and rocks and old wasp nests and that robin's nest one time."

"And the toad he found in the driveway. He was so happy he saved it from being run over."

"And then he asked me to wash it because it looked so dirty."

"I bet," said Cassie, "he might have been a scientist when he grew up."

Tears were filling my eyes again.

"Remember Mom and the snake?" I started to say more but then I couldn't talk.

Cassie nodded. Of course she remembered.

"We were picking blackberries," she said. "And she reached into a bush and suddenly she gave this funny little yelp and dropped her bucket. And blackberries went rolling all over and Mom said, 'Don't move, children. It's a snake.'"

"Right. And of course we all dropped our buckets too. And then she looked again and it turned out it wasn't a snake at all but just a piece of garden hose that somehow got lost in the bushes."

"And we tried to pick up those berries but half of them were squashed and we only had enough that year to make tarts instead of a pie."

We sat there smiling and crying and all at once I was so tired I felt like going home.

But Cassie said, "We have to finish picking."

She was right. "Yes," I said.

So we did. We picked blackberries until we were so hot and sticky and purple all over that we couldn't stand it.

Then we walked home and made a pie.

The crust was a disaster. But my father said the blackberries were delicious.

thirty-one...

Lucy came again.

She came when I had the dreams. The ones where I am flying and then falling. The ones where my mother and Ben are with me and I am so happy but then they disappear and I walk around searching and searching but I can't find them anywhere.

The ones where I wake up crying.

Lucy would come and sit close to me on my bed and hold me. "It's all right," she would whisper over and over.

And slowly I would calm down and after a long time it would be all right.

Sometimes she sang to me. Those baby songs my mother used to sing when I was little that made me feel safe and warm. Now I know why they are called lulla-bies. Lucy would lull me back to sleep with her soft songs.

Sometimes we played cards sitting cross-legged on my bed. Lucy was a mean cardplayer. Fast and tricky and she played to win slapping down those cards *smack smack*. If I happened to beat her those dark eyes looked so disappointed I had to smile.

I told her about Douglas. Lucy listened and nodded her big head and didn't say anything and that was fine.

Summer dribbled away and just like that one day it was fall.

School started and my new teacher was Mr. Carlisle who was so much nicer than Mrs. Deeley it was like he'd been given to me as a reward for a year of suffering.

Isabelle wasn't in my class but we had lunch together every day.

I had her mom cut my hair at her beauty shop and she told me what to do about the frizz. I went to the drug-store and bought some special hair stuff that cost a fortune and it worked.

Cassie passed her driving test. She parallel-parked perfectly, only after that she didn't see a Stop sign and didn't stop but she passed anyway. All of a sudden she will take me anywhere as long as she gets to drive. Some days she even drives me to school.

Alexander went to a playoff game but he didn't get another real Yankee baseball. He is starting to play football now wearing his green Jets shirt and helmet that his mother bought.

One night in October I was lying in bed feeling the way you do when it is cool outside but you are curled up nice and cozy under your quilt. A fat moon was rising over the trees streaming light in through the window. Lucy was there stretched out across the bottom of the bed keeping my feet warm.

My eyes closed. I was drifting slowly into sleep when I felt something change.

My eyes blinked open.

Lucy stood next to the window looking out. Her front paws were up on the windowsill. The moonlight made her fur look silvery. Her nose twitched as she sniffed the air.

"Lucy," I said.

She looked back at me for just a moment. Then she jumped.

Out the window into the dark sky.

"Lucy!" I called.

She never came back.

But she is still with me. Always.